RISING DARKNESS

Book 2 of The Enchantment

J. Michael McFadden

ARGON PRESS

ii   *J. Michael McFadden*

Published in the United States of America by Argon Press
ISBN-13 (CS print): 978-1-944815-72-1

Version 1.2.7

Dedication

To my "Hogwarts" Grandson,

Owen Andrew McFadden

Table of Contents

Cast of Characters

Deidre... 9-year-old 1ˢᵗ millennium Irish girl

Culain...10-year-old best friend of Deidre

Abbess Brigit...Mentor of Deidre and Culain

Abbess Margaret...Brigit's sister

Angus...Abbey monk, scribe

Ankara...Ancient Oak Sentinel of the Enchanted Forest

Brugh Donn...Milesian invader

Caleb and Martha...Deidre's Da and Mum

Conchubar...King of Ulster

Colin McGee...Cauldron maker

Ermanci...Shapeshifting pirate captain

Gabrielle...Faerie voice of Deidre's heart

Isis...Banshee faerie

Laegaire...King's Court Enchanter

Maeve...Queen of the Faeries

Lugh...The magical piper, Light-bearer

Macha...Queen of Ulster

Milesians...Sons of Mil, invaders

Morici...Former Dark Queen Enchantress of the Donns

Morgana...Banshee faerie

Morgar...Dark Enchanter

Nacham...Faerie voice of Deidre's reason

Nog...Faerie voice of Culain's reason

Osiris...Oak Sentinel of the Banshee Gate

Sultain...King's Protector

Places in The Enchantment Saga

Emerald Isle...Ireland
Eire... both island and its goddess
Spain...earlier home of the Milesians

Ulster...Irish Province, Deidre's home, c. 1000
Boar's Inn... home of Deidre, Caleb and Martha
Ards Abbey...home of Abbess Brigit and Angus
Ards Forest...Enchanted Forest near Boar's Inn
Doe Castle...home of King and Queen of Ulster
And Milesian Brugh Donn
Doe Abbey...home of Abbess Margaret
St. Michael the Archangel...Fr. Malachy's church

The Enchantment...Magical Realm of faeries, descendants of the Tuatha De Danann
Faerie Sand Castle... home to faeries, leprechauns
deep within the Ards Forest
First Gate...magical shaft Deidre falls through in
her first trip into the Enchantment
Banshee Gate...magical second entrance from Eire
through the banshee forest
Oval Gate... third and largest entrance from Eire
into the Ards Forest Enchantment
Veritas... river of Enchantment

Other Books

Deidre's Dawn
Book 1 of The Enchantment

Star Lights
Book 3 of The Enchantment
Releases in 2019

Chapter 1

Retreat

 ulain will slide to his death if he loses his footing from the steep edge of the cliff. He shows no concern for risk as he scans the horizon with palm saluting above his forehead. He looks older, wiser. I suppose I do, too. But I sit back on a log, nursing the pain of purpling bruises. I rub some of Colin's green balm on my throbbing knee. I sigh at its cool, soothing touch. When I look up, Culain is gone. A chill makes the hair on my arms stand on end. I do not call out for fear of alerting Brugh Donn's warriors, but my eyes scan the distance as I step cautiously closer to the cliff's sharp edge.

"Culain!" It comes out as a loud whisper, but with no response. I stoop to my knees and look over the edge as my pulse races. Only dizzying depth and crashing surf. No sign of Culain. I pull back on my haunches and take a deep breath.

The sun warmly basks my face, but this is no Enchantment. Its texture is dull and muted. I miss the showering vibrancy. Queen Maeve is nowhere to counsel me. Colin and the fairies and leprechauns cannot support me with their ministries. And Culain. Where is he? I feel even more alone than at Emerald Mountain.

A reflected light flashes at me from the edge of oaks. As I draw closer, I see only a puddle of water rustling in the breeze. I sit down and gaze into the pool's glassy surface. I pull back as a tear wells up in my eye. No. Not me. I look again. The swelling on my right forehead has turned a yellowish purple. Stains of blood and mud cake my face like a ghoulish mask. My hair looks like seaweed. The tear slowly moistens some blood and makes it redden. No wonder my parents did not know me at the castle. I don't even recognize myself. New tears spread as I recall their re-capture. Maybe they are dead.

"Deidre!" I hear the whisper, but my searching eyes find no source.

"Wipe your face with our water, Deidre." I see a brief ripple of an eye as it winks at me from the wide oak next to the water. The voice reminds me of my oak friends in the Enchantment, Ankara and Osiris. I need no urging. Even though the water I splash is muddy with the rich darkness of turf, its refreshing magic surprises me. I continue to believe in the power of enchantment. As the ripples fade to a glassy mirror surface, my reflection looks like the real me, despite the still discolored forehead. As the tears, blood, and dirt wash away so do my doubts, fears, and sadness.

I feel a hand on my shoulder. Startled, I pull away quickly, rolling onto the ground with one hand splashing in the water. Then I giggle. Culain stands there, hands on his hips, smiling at me. Laughing feels as cleansing as the water. Culain strides toward me, offering a hand to help me up. I cannot resist pulling him down toward me. His rear plops solidly in the puddle with a gooshy splash. I let go of his hand and run toward camp. He smiles as he chases me. My pains do not bother me as I run.

I squeal as he catches me from behind. He wipes some of the oak water in my hair.

"I baptize you in the name of the Oak." We both smile and simply enjoy one of the brief respites of levity.

"Culain, your baptism was quite enchanting!" My friend turns his back to me and sways his dripping rump. I give it a friendly swat and sprinkle wetness over his blonde top.

"Your baptism is now complete!" We both fall to the ground laughing like drunken sailors. Then we hear other laughter.

It is the oaks around us. This is an enchanting gift, a refreshing baptism, a rite of initiation into the natural spirit of the Oak. We each run to the nearest oak and pat them fondly.

Then the sky darkens and the wind rises with a quiet chill. The reality of our plight hits me like a slap. Laegaire is on a scouting mission. Morici has suddenly disappeared in the woods. The Abbesses are gone to pick berries for us. So here we are, two children alone with Brugh Donn's forces likely searching for us. Morici's magic surely could protect us, but she is nowhere to be seen. Culain and I have enchanted swords, but we do not know if they work outside the Enchanted Ards Forest. My belly tightens.

"I'm getting worried, Culain." The winds whip stronger and the skies darken. As a crow shrieks, I instinctively back into Culain and watch dark birds approach.

"Relax, Deidre. Crows are a good sign for us. They're Morici's messengers and now she's our friend." Still, chills travel up my spine.

A voice whispers in the wind. "Trust Culain." It is Gabrielle, my heart faerie. My muscles soften and I squeeze Culain's arm.

"Thanks. You're right."

Then a host of crows circle above, darting and screeching as though they are anything but friends. We retreat to a broad, skyscraping oak.

A hand reaches around the oak and grabs my shoulder. I scream instinctively. Culain pulls out his sword. It flashes sparks as the birds squeal away.

"They're harmless." Morici extends her hands with an object that makes us catch our breath. The Book of Invasions! The same Angus manuscript that we took from the abbey. The curling Angus A in the lower right-hand corner is unmistakable.

"Send them away, Morici, they will call attention to us." Morici rolls back her eyes.

"Your inexperience shows, Culain. These crows of mine have told me that we are safe here. They are the best scouts we could possibly have. No warriors are within miles of here. But look at this manuscript."

"It's ours!" I feel and sound very possessive.

"Deidre, it belongs to the abbey. Remember, we only borrowed it." Culain is so irritatingly right sometimes. He turns to Morici and continues as he takes the book and flips its pages.

"Deidre carried it with us in the carriage, but we

thought it was lost in the crash. Where did you find it?"

Morici paces around the oak. "Lugh gave it me."

"Lugh!" We both look at each other at once.

When we look back, Morici and the crows are gone again.

Culain looks up from the book with a reassuring smile.

"The House of Donn are a strange lot, Deidre, but Lugh has entrusted Morici with this manuscript. Only Lugh could have done this. Sit down and read from it to me."

As he passes it, I hear familiar sounds in the distance. The distinctive flute music of Lugh. It calms me. I smile and Culain returns the grin. I sit down on the grassy carpet of an emerald clearing. Culain and I cross our legs as the sun's rays warm us. As the music fades, I notice something different about the book. There is a red cloth page marker woven into the binding. As I open the page it marks, I gasp at the crest, the Conall crest, my father's crest. I show it to Culain.

"It must mark something important, Deeder. Read it." I had told Culain to stop calling me Deeder. I was 9 now after all. But I knew it was a sign of affection, so I let it pass without comment.

The manuscript pages following the red marker are new. The writing looks like that of Angus, but I cannot be sure. It is the story of Culain and me at Doe Castle. I draw in my breath and put my hand to my mouth. I finally exhale and begin to read aloud as Culain patiently waits.

"The young princess Deidre successfully broke the dark spell that ruled the life of Morici, enchantress of the House of Donn. She became an ally to the fledgling cause to return power to the rightful king, to honor the call of Tara. The High King's liege, Sultain, was released from his chains to rejoin his son, Culain. They joined Morici in freeing the royal couple, but King Conchubar and Queen Macha were weak and deluded by Brugh Donn, and did not recognize their daughter. The rebels broke through Brugh Donn's guard, escaping to the nearby forest, but the king and queen were held in custody..."

"Culain, they are only held in custody! They are alive! We can still save them!" I rise as I speak and circle Culain so that he looks almost dizzy as he tries to follow me. He grabs my arm and pulls me back to the earth.

"Quiet, now! We need to stay hidden. I agree. The crest proves that they're still alive. We need a plan before we return. Patience, Deeder!"

The words and the ground soothe my racing heart. My breathing slows.

"Where are the others?"

As though the forest hears me, Morici reappears, running quickly.

"He's coming on horseback." She points to a narrow path. The rapid cloppety-clop of a rider draws closer. A neigh rises from his magnificent white steed. It's wide thighs ripple with strength as it tears turf up like thunderbolts. The rider's hood is drawn by strings to his head and billows like a sail. His cape makes him look like a dark angel flapping his wings. Overhead, the crows accompany the rider like silent sentinels. He pulls up abruptly in front of us and dismounts like a knight in his prime. But the shadowy features are undeniable.

"Laegaire!" We chime in unison.

The smile on his face fills us with hope. The strength of his riding encourages us. He speaks quickly, demanding attention as he quiets his horse.

"The Resistance is rising. The word is spreading in Ulster that the true High King has returned to strength and will retake his rightful throne now that Morici has abandoned Doe Castle."

"Will Brugh Donn try to kill my father?" I had to ask.

"He's no fool. With the word spreading that the High King will return to power, Brugh Donn risks open revolt if he harms the king or queen. They're safe for now."

I pat the manuscript and look at Culain. With a knowing glance, he grabs my hand and holds it reassuringly.

"All of you have performed well in this. I have spread the word to old allies of the king. We must stand together until the Old Guard re-gathers. Like King Conchubar they have lost heart. But they have heard of Deidre and Culain's breach of Doe Castle. It inspires them."

He pats us on the head and turns to Morici with crows on her shoulder and tiredness in her eyes.

"I never thought a Court Enchanter with such dark power could change, Morici. But I have seen you with my eyes and my heart. The princess has touched you and you have become a true daughter of Eire and a supporter of Danu. I salute you."

He removes his sword, which sparkles in the sun and rests it gently on each of her shoulders as the dark birds fly aloft.

"I welcome you to the Order of Danu, the realm of the Tuatha, the light of Lugh."

Tears forms in her eyes. She kneels before Laegaire.

"Forgive me for all my lies and plotting. I was blind to the truth."

I run and hug her. Culain joins me.

"Morici, now it is only you who need to forgive yourself."

Then we hear the scuffle of skirts as the two abbesses appear with nuts, berries, and a pheasant in hand. Bridget drops her bow to the ground and smiles at us.

"What kind of resistance can we be if we don't

eat? What do you think, Laegaire, can we build a fire?"

He laughs at this earthy woman's assertiveness. He points to the crows.

"You're scaring the birds, Abbess! You'd better ask Morici for the answer to your question."

The rising Morici nods. "Brugh Donn's troops are many miles away. They're returning to the castle. It grows dusk. It's safe to build a fire."

Culain and I begin to gather sticks and branches inside a ring of rocks. The abbesses and Laegaire help us, but Morici stands her ground and looks above at the darkening sky. She watches the smoke rise from our crackling kindling that Laegaire ignites as sparks from his sword strike rock like a flint. The shadows dance across Morici's face, revealing tight, intense features.

"Do you think they'll see our smoke?" Although encouraged by Laegaire, I still feel cautious. I sense Nacham, my faerie of reason, stirring my doubts. Is this worrying Morici?

"No, Deidre, it's not that. The crows are uneasy. Not from the abbesses' fire. A new threat is coming but isn't yet here. They sense it."

Morici turns to Laegaire. "There's more. What are you keeping from us?"

Laegaire steps back from the now rising flames, creating a caped silhouette in the rising darkness. I cannot see his expression. Silence surrounds the crackles of the fire. All eyes are upon the statue-like Enchanter. He pulls back his hood and looks in the core of the crimson flames. He throws reflecting dust into the heat. It explodes into purple sparkles that press back the rest of us. We all take in our breaths as Laegaire calmly holds his ground and turns to us.

"An ancient Enchanter of dark magic draws near. He will take Morici's place at Brugh Donn's side. His magic is very dark."

The force of new bursts of purple pushes us back further. I begin to tremble.

"Who is it, Laegaire?"

He looks at Morici, coldly.

"You know, don't you?"

Her face is blank of any emotion. She says nothing, turns, and walks into the darkening woods. The agitated crows circle around her and blend into the darkness.

I feel a shiver, but dare not get closer to the fire where hazy, violet blasts still burst. Culain puts his arm around me as he sees me trembling from the cool evening mist and the specter of a new enemy. The moon bursts out from its cloudy blanket to show its full roundness. A howl rises from the deep woods. Dark omens.

As Laegaire returns his gaze to the fire, the manuscript lays open with a royal crest glittering from its red cloth marker. He rushes over to it.

"Deidre, where did you find this?" His eyes burn intensely.

I look in the direction where Morici left us. I point there. "Lugh gave it to her." His eyes widen.

"This manuscript was touched by Lugh. There may be changes that will give us clues in aiding the King." He thrusts the book into my hands. "Start reading from the new page, Deidre." I rush to read the last paragraph, but I know Laegaire wants to start with the story of yesterday. The abbesses bustle about preparing food over the crackling fire while I read. The pungent aroma of burning wood is sweetened by the savory smell of grilling pheasant. Laegaire paces in the shadows. Culain tends the fire, adding twigs and fallen branches. The smoke burns my eyes. I cough, but rush into the reading.

"The princess Deidre thawed the thick icy masks of defeat and sorrow that hardened the minds and hearts of Conchubar and Macha. This was possible only with the assistance of her new ally, Morici. For Morici had used her powers to imprison them. Only through her could they be truly released to know their daughter again."

My voice trembles and stops. The memory is vivid. How hard it was to have my parents turn away from me with their icy visages and slumped shoulders. Morici had appealed to them, disarmed them of their doubt. The very sower of doubt dispelled it. I feel an arm on my shoulder. It is Morici. I cover her hand gently with mine and look at her as small tears trickle down my cheek. Her often-grim look is now soft. I feel reassured that she is with us and that Laegaire affirms her as an ally.

"Continue, Deidre. As Laegaire said, there may be clues."

I take a deep breath and look across the fire to the Abbesses and Culain. They smile reassuringly. Laegaire stands still, arms crossed, hidden in the shadows like a dark sentry. I feel secure and re-open the page.

"As the royal family celebrated their reunion, Brugh Donn and his guards stormed the room. Sultain, swordless, began swinging the chains still clasped to his arms at the oncoming swords. Brugh Donn slashed him on the side of his calf, crumpling him to the ground. With the shout, more of a man than a boy, young Culain produced his sword and shattered Brugh Donn's sword in a single blow, as the ice-masked usurper fell to the ground holding his wrist in pain. The swell of soldiers thrust toward Culain, but he shattered swords with ease and grace. Several escaped him and seized the king and queen and took them out a door before anyone could aid them. Laegaire joined Culain in the battle. Brugh Donn picked up a battle axe and was about to strike Culain from behind, but Morici struck him with a bolt of lightning, sending him and his metal crashing to the ground in a heap."

I need to stop reading. It feels too present. I remember the abbesses pulling me into the corner. The soldiers ignored the women and a girl. I remember how my heart fell as I saw Brugh Donn about to strike Culain. Brugh Donn's face and body were so covered with a crusty ice that he looked invincible, but Morici's strike was powerful and quick. It was not recorded in the book, but I recall her words.

"Brugh Donn, the venom of vengeance poisons you. Until you take the antidote, I will use my powers to defeat you."

I remember that she had guided the rest of the women out of the back entrance, entrusting the remaining battle to Culain and Laegaire. As these memories stir in my mind, I sense a growing curiosity about how that battle went.

"Deeder, continue." Culain is growing impatient with my pauses. I return my eyes to where my finger holds the place and put the book closer to the fire for light.

"Morici threw several more strikes of lightning in the direction of the soldiers. Several were knocked to the ground and some fled. But the honor guard held their ground. Morici led the princess and the abbesses out the back, where the king and queen had been taken. Sultain remained on the floor as blood flowed from his wound. Laegaire transformed himself into an eagle and used his talons to tear at the wrists of the guard. Young Culain was the lone swordsman. He shattered every sword and every icy shield that remained of the guard. Culain defeated three dozen men in this battle. This would be the first triumph of the Champion of Ulster."

I read it, but I cannot believe it. Culain, my Culain, the Champion of Ulster! He is just a boy. I stop and look at him.

"Is this true, Culain?" He is silent and walks away into the shadows. Laegaire steps forward into the light and speaks quietly but firmly mostly for me to hear.

"It was foretold that a great champion would rise in Ulster to defend the Tuatha De Danaan and its kingdom within Ulster from all usurpers. The prophecy predicted his prowess in battle as a child. Culain is the one."

I gasp despite myself. Laegaire lays his index finger firmly in front of his lips. "Speak no more of this prophecy."

"Time to eat!" Both Abbess Brigit and Margaret proclaim at once. The aroma of pheasant brings rumbles to our stomachs. There is more to read, but I sense that we know enough now. The berries they pass around in a satchel are sweet. The meat is greasy and hot as we pick it apart with our hands. Laegaire passes around the leather skin bladder that holds fresh water from the river.

As we lick our fingers, Laegaire stands in front of the fire. His silhouette rises larger with sparks and crackles of fire behind him. I cannot see his expression, but his voice is stern.

"We engaged Brugh Donn and his inner guard and soldiers with success thanks to Culain and Morici especially, but as we escaped we had to leave Sultain behind. He was bleeding too badly to move him. I have learned through the Resistance that he remains alive and recovering, back in his prison cell."

Laegaire glances in the direction of Culain who

remains in the shadows.

"Brugh Donn knows that we won't abandon Sultain or the royal couple. He has the upper hand. He doesn't need to come after us."

Abbess Brigit shuffles her skirts forward.

"So, they use them as bait to lure us back."

"Yes, Abbess, I am afraid so."

I chip in. "Did my reading give you any clues as to how we might save my parents and Sultain?"

Laegaire looks in the night's darkness, and despite his own directive to me, speaks firmly.

"We have the Champion of Ulster."

A familiar female voice comes from the shadows.

"And they have the Dark Enchanter." Then Morici drifts further into the thickening darkness. I shiver with a chill.

Chapter 2

A Darker Enchanter

 aegaire may call for silence about the Champion of Ulster, but I cannot wait any longer. As Culain stokes the fire with a piece of wood, I grab his wrist. He drops the pointed stick into the embers and a stream of red flashes dance like a faerie. I pull him near the oaks and we sit amid the gnarly roots of the stoutest tree.

"What really happened back at Doe Castle?"

"Just as you read from the Book of Invasions." He is not convincing me.

"Did you kill them?"

He grabs my shoulders firmly and looks steadily into my eyes.

"I, like you, bear the sword of Lugh, the sword of

Light. It does not kill human life. It destroys darkness. It melts hearts." His gaze is hot like the fire. His words ring true to me. He releases my shoulders. But I immediately grip his like talons upon prey.

"Then tell me what happened--the whole story" My eyes match the heat of his gaze. I release my grip.

He sits still for a moment and rests his legs against the thick roots. We feel the gentle but strong presence of the Oak.

"It is much as you remember with Morici. Whenever I use my sword, it only sizzles and melts the icy armor that people choose to encase themselves with, thinking it protects them. I also can shatter swords and metal armor, but killing -- never."

"What happened to them?"

"With their armor and ice gone, they felt vulnerable and weak. They did not know how to act. They just ran away."

"So Brugh Donn's full guard remains?"

"No, Deidre. They ran away completely. They can revert to fear and coldness – but not soon. They are useless to Brugh Donn for now."

I feel relieved. I also feel awe at the Champion of Ulster. He does not slay men, as the heroes of other epics.

He slays the icy hardness of heart that stifles them. He casts out their darkness with the light of Lugh's sword.

Robes rustle nearby. The Abbess kneels beside us.

"Children, the power of Lugh's sword is greater than any other. But only if you place your full trust in it and listen to your hearts. Never use the sword with malice or revenge. If you do, it will cease to serve you."

She pats us both lovingly upon the head.

"The two of you are the hope of all Eire. The fears and vengefulness of the Milesians have darkened the land. Their lust for power and wealth and the fear of losing it has spread a dark web throughout the kingdom."

I do not see her face at first, but I had felt her approach and sensed her presence. Her voice reassures me, but words of a dark web quicken my pulse and bring a bead of sweat to my brow.

"Deidre, even your father, the High King, with all his skill yielded to the power of fear, his fear of losing you. He lost his trust in the power of Enchantment. He's regaining it with your help."

Culain stands up.

"And Morici's."

"Yes, Culain. Morici allowed the loving energy of

Deidre's sword to touch her heart and transform her. But this still is a time of testing for her. The old patterns of revenge run deep in Morici's blood. She can choose to continue or to reject them. But they will test her. She needs our support. Do you understand?"

We both nod. All three of us sit silently for a while. Then I hug Culain. "Thank you for your valor at Doe Castle. Thanks for being our champion."

Before I finish, the abbess joins in our hug.

Then Culain shudders a little and sobs. We hold him tightly. The Abbess consoles him.

"Sultain will live, young Culain. He is strong, like you. Trust in the power of Enchantment."

The words feel like a balm to the emotions. My own tears of empathy for Sultain stop. But then, the thought of my parents returns. I was only with them for fleeting moments. I miss them again. My chest heaves.

"We will release them, Deeder!" The words are so confident that I catch my breath. The endearing Deeder feels just right. My trust grows. I hear a whisper in both ears. Both Gabrielle and Nacham speak the same message.

"Trust the Enchantment!"

As I break free of the embrace, I stand tall upon a

stone. I feel a rush of strength and energy fill me.

"We must find Queen Maeve and seek advice at the Sand Castle in the Enchanted Forest!" The words simply rise in me without thought.

The Abbess Margaret approaches us.

"Deidre gives wise counsel, Brigit. Wouldn't you agree?" She hikes her broad skirts as she climbs over oak roots.

Brigit nods as a hand rests upon her shoulder. Margaret's fiery eyes are unmistakable beneath a brimming hood.

"In the morning, we head to the Ards Forest to find the gate to the Enchantment and Queen Maeve."

Maeve will help us. My confidence grows.

A sudden flutter of wings arises overhead. Only the sound of an occasional screech belies their presence and their leader.

"Quick! Over here." Morici's voice comes from well beyond the other side of the fire. Laegaire grabs the cool end of a burning log and holds it in front of us as we stride quickly in the direction of Morici.

A pained moan arises ahead. A man's moan. The man gives a weak cry.

"Help me." The voice is but a whisper.

Culain rushes ahead of us all like the wind. "Father, I'm coming." As we approach, Morici is gently lowering Sultain to the ground. Laegaire's torch lights up the crimson bandage around his calf. Sultain's face is ashen. Culain cradles his father's head in his lap and brushes back his hair. Margaret immediately tends to the wound. Brigit hands her some balm and leaves from the medicine pouch that dangles from her robes. Laegaire scatters some faerie dust about and I find the water pouch. Morici, tired and out of breath, sits. We all attend to various duties before setting a blanket in front of the fire to warm it for Sultain. He is beginning to shiver and shake. He welcomes the heated cover. Culain's tears drip onto his father's forehead. All honor them with quiet.

Once Sultain falls into a healing sleep, Laegaire gathers us about the fire and speaks in whispering tones, occasionally pointing a direction with his staff. His misty white beard glistens in the fire's reflection. He is our most trusted leader, the Court Enchanter of the High King. We listen with rapt attention.

"Morici, how did you come upon Sultain?"

"I shape-shifted into one of my crows and flew to Doe Castle. Conchubar and Macha are safe. They're gathering strength. Many of Brugh Donn's guards have fled." She glanced at Culain watching quietly over his father, holding his hand.

"Sultain was left for dead. I could not bear to leave him there. I distracted the guards with my crows, and put him in a wheel barrow and carried him away. His wounds fester." The abbesses nod silently with lowered heads. I glance and see the pain in Culain's eyes.

With a heavy heart, Morici continues, "We need courage. My replacement brings fresh warriors within days. Like me, he is a shape-shifter. His own inner guards also are shape-shifters. Their favorite form is the hawk."

One of the crows that always circle Morici lands in front of the fire. A dervish of mist and smoke swirl into a growing cocoon around the bird. Then a face emerges, much like a Saracen pirate with dark hair, a jet-black beard, and a black patch over one eye. The colorful bandana about his head contrasts to the dark brown, green, and grey of the forest. His broad shoulders are tattooed with exotic birds and he brandishes a sword that looks like a scythe.

"Welcome Ermanci, the captain of my sailing vessel. He heads the crew that flies about us. He only can shift his shape during the night. But the Dark Enchanter brings more like Ermanci."

There is a hush among us, especially as Ermanci

steps forward, fully 7 feet tall with a great black mustache. His image is menacing even though he bears no armor, save a small breastplate. He bows to all of us with a respectful flourish.

"At yer service, amigos." His Spanish accent rings clear.

Laegaire is unimpressed by Ermanci's appearance.

"Morici, did you learn anything else at Doe Castle?" The Spaniard stretches his long legs on the ground and several of the crows came to roost on his shoulders.

"As I was saying, me successor as court enchanter will have the same shape-shifters at his command. But they are no less trained that mine."

"Morici, you and Sultain escaped too easily. Were you followed?" Laegaire sounds irritated, concerned that Morici may have put us in danger.

Waving her hands down to hush the conversation, Morici whispers, "Sultain does not have much time left. Brugh Donn knew. He hopes to bait revenge, especially from Culain." She turns briefly to make sure we are not overheard. I look to at my friend, holding his father's hand. Tears well in my eyes, touched by his pain.

Laegaire sighs and clenches his hands together. "Thank you, Morici, for bringing Sultain to us. We will minister to him. But we must prepare ourselves to split up."

I gasp out loud. "No, we must stay together!"

"Dear Deidre, I must go and work with the local Resistance. You and Culain must go to Queen Maeve in the Enchantment to get reinforcements and guidance on how to deal with the Dark Enchanter. The abbesses cannot enter the Enchanted Forest. Certainly, Morici, the Oak will not allow you to enter after your defeat at Emerald Mountain. It will be up to you two to get the help we need."

Culain has just sat down to join us, gazing back toward Sultain. I can tell he has heard Laegaire's plan to split up, but he sits quietly.

As Laegaire spoke it made sense, but as I realize that I must travel back without any grown-ups, my heart begins to waver. I hear Nacham's voice.

"Don't head back without least a guard like Ermanci." Since I am the only one to hear this faerie voice, I speak up. "Can we take the giant?"

Culain sighs. "I must stay with my father. Do send Ermanci with Deeder." My heart sinks. I cannot imagine being without at least Culain and the Spanish pirate.

Laegaire stands up, strides firmly and strikes his staff into the fire, stoking embers and sparkling the air with what look like thousands of fireflies. His face looks grizzled and set.

"We have no choice. Since this new dark enchanter has powers equal to Morici, we have a challenge on our hands. Culain, Morici and her crew will guard and care for Sultain. Spend time with your father tonight, Culain. Then you and Deidre must return to Maeve and get reinforcements, maybe the banshees. I will trust you two. I will take the abbesses with me to gather local support." Culain sits still, saying nothing. I can see that he will not leave his father -- and he walks over to him. Laegaire, I think, senses that the end is near for Sultain. I join my friend at his father's side. Higher powers than any of us will guide our destiny.

Morici's crows begin to squawk and dart around as though telling us to move. Unexpectedly a barrage of flaming arrows strike and some pierce the ground, throwing sparks and red embers. A sliver of burning ash lands on the open Book of Invasions. Against Culain's tug, I break free and grab it as an arrow pierces my frock, pinning me to an oak until I rip it free. Then I pull out my sword of Lugh and begin deflecting arrows with a skill that startles even me. Culain stays firmly in front of Sultain, deflecting arrows as though they are mosquitoes. Laegaire comes to my side. Ermanci charges in the direction of the attackers and shouts of fear can already be heard in the distance. The arrows stop. Ermanci returns to the firelight with lockets of hair cut from his foes that now run, squealing in the distance. His sword is free of blood, but an arrow pierces his arm. As he drops the locks of hair into the fire, he falls, thundering to the ground. I shiver. Morici brings salve to nurse him. The abbesses bring cloths to bandage him. Several crows hover over Ermanci and Morici. The former dark queen listens to the voices of her emissaries.

"It's just an isolated roving band of the honor guard, some hotheads out for glory. They won't return tonight, but we must leave before sunrise. We had best put out the fire."

As she looks at Culain, he demands. "Sultain comes with us."

Abbess Margaret puts her arms around Culain. It calms him. Morici is silent. I put my hand on his shoulder. Once my friend's emotion softens, Margaret tends to Sultain's calf wounds. The other Abbess checks Ermanci's shoulder.

Although Morici's scouts failed to find this one band, Ermanci's courage and defense of the camp proves their allegiance to us. I begin to shovel some dirt over the fire to smother it. Laegaire motions to me.

"Stand back, Deidre."

He raises his arms and extends his staff.   A whirling stream of leaves and grass begin to spin in front of him and grow in strength like a small tornado.   He directs it to the fire and quenches it as easily as extinguishing a candle with a brass snuffer.

"My friends, I beg all of you to rest. I will stand watch until sunrise approaches. Then we all must depart on our separate journeys." The request is met by an approving silence, although Culain holds his father's hand tightly, saying nothing. I doubt that he will follow his orders. I find a spot next to Morici, near the large Oak. She wraps her shawl around both of us. I whisper one last question to her.

"Who's this dark enchanter who replaces you?"

"My teacher in the magical arts, Deidre."

"What's his name?"

She whispers the response. "Morgar. I speak it softly to avoid giving him power."

"Is he as dark as you were before you chose to

change?"

"More so. I know as well as anyone."

"Because he was your teacher?"

"Because he's my father."

I do not feel afraid for her or for us, but a deep sadness wells up in me and comes out as tears, tears of love for her and her endurance of such a father. My complaints about Caleb feel very small. We hug each other until sleep overcomes us.

J. Michael McFadden

Chapter 3

Darkness Rises

 greet the sunrise with a close-eyed yawn. As I brush the grass, it slides with dew and I smell the musk of clover. Then it hits me like a blow to the chest. Laegaire is not by the fire. He was to call us to depart before dawn. His staff lays idle and he sleeps with his head atop his tattered hood. I shiver in the morning breeze. What spell draws him from his post? Then Morici stirs. I see the same alarm in her eyes that I feel. She bids me silence with a finger to her lips, gently unwraps me from her shawl and marches toward Laegaire. She scans skies and treetops. It is what she does not see that concerns her. No black crows. Save the shape-shifted Spaniard, Ermanci, who rests comfortably next to

Sultain. It may be Morici or his sixth sense of his missing crew, but Ermanci's head pops up. *Holding his shoulder, he shuffles toward Morici as I wrap the shawl more tightly around me.* *My mouth is dry and my heart paces faster.*

Both Morici and Ermanci whip their eyes toward Doe Castle. I sense nothing. A distant sound pierces the quiet, a muffled cry, a bird in trouble. As the cries grow closer, others awake one by one. First Culain. Then Abbess Brigit. Strangely Laegaire remains asleep. The cry of the birds makes my heart flutter. I scan the treetops without reward.

Morici startles Laegaire with a hard push. "Wake up, Enchanter! The enemy is nearly upon us." Swords appear. The Abbess pulls me back, but I break free and pull out my sword. Everyone looks toward the rising screeches. A crow with wounds lands at Morici's feet. My mouth grows drier and my tummy feels at sea. Two more of her crew appear -- tattered, wounded by some marauder. Ermanci's eyes fill with tears. His friends have died in serving us. I empathize Ermanci's loss, but there is not much time for feeling. We see them. Hawks! Large, swift, screeching. Dozens. Black feathers in their talons. Surely scouts of the Dark Enchanter. Their fierce agility easily overmatches the crows. They swoop in on us, looking for the weakest.

They think that is me -- their biggest mistake! My anger trumps my fears. I stand next to Culain, protecting Sultain. Sultain holds a sword, but he cannot stand alone. As a lead hawk swoops towards me, I thrust Lugh forward. Sparks dance from the tip of the blade and rise in multiplying volleys, knocking the bird from his flight and forcing back the dozen behind him. The smoky aroma of sparks exhilarates me and I step forward. The lead hawk is bigger and carries a shiny object with a chain in its beak. As more sparks hit, it drops the pendant-like piece to the ground. I pay little notice, but feel a deep desire to look back at it. Another group of marauders approach from the other side, but Culain hurls them the same medicine. His eyes are intense and bright. Laegaire throws an even wider spray from his sword to repel the remaining horde. The crows' fate will not be ours. I am flush with energy from the fray, almost taunting more hawks with my brandished sword. Culain gently lowers my arm pointing to Morici and Ermanci who tend to wounded dark birds. I take a deep breath and taste the morning air and recall the shiny object that fell from the sky. I scan the field until its reflection glistens at me. It looks like an amulet.

"What cursed spell came over me!" Laegaire is furious that he had not set us off before the rising sun.

"It's Morgar. He's nearby. In the dark of night,

he can cast a sleeping spell -- even on enchanters."
Morici's words bring a chill to my spine. Fear returns to
my chest and my breath grows shallow as sweat beads on
my palms. I worry that Morgar can pull such a trick on
Laegaire. I look around suspiciously. As I lift the amulet,
it feels heavier and heavier as though it knows my worry.

"Stop, Deidre! That's Morgar's amulet." Morici
sounds frightened.

The weight now almost drags me down to the
ground as I struggle to prevent it slipping from my sweaty
hand. Morici grabs at the identical amulet about her neck
and screams. The dark blue center of each amulet turns
blood red. Both steam with heat. As I feel the burn sizzle
my skin, I drop mine with a squeal. My hand glows with
red and I rub it across the wet dew. Morici clutches at hers
and throws it off, her hands and neck crimson with burns.
I am in pain and afraid. I strike at the amulet in anger with
my sword but it pushes me back. Both amulets are only a
few yards apart. Culain rushes between them. Despite
protests from both Morici and me, he calmly puts both
amulets about his neck and begins to play Lugh's tune
with his flute. Somehow, he is immune to the heat and
soon the amulet's color softens to blue. I breathe easier,
my shoulders drop and I take another brush across the
sweet dew.

It hits me. Culain is an Enchanter as well as a Champion. Who is this friend of mine? Not just a simple Irish lad. Despite my burning hand, I feel a fond pride in my best friend.

Laegaire again is impatient. "Enough music, lad. The shape-shifter that lost his amulet will soon be back. Give them to me." But as soon as Laegaire touches them, they began to steam again and he drops them to the ground.

"What power has this Morgar?" Laegaire looks furtively about for more signs. Culain begins to play his flute again and hands the amulets to Laegaire. Then he pulls out some faery dust with a purple hue and sprinkles them over the blue surface. Soon small sparks pop and the amulets' color drains out like sand. Culain stops his music. His magic gives me goose bumps.

"Lugh has the power over all amulets, Laegaire. He taught me this. Here is some of the lavender faerie dust of Lugh." Laegaire does not look completely pleased by his student outshining him, but he pats my friend on the head. I smile inwardly at Culain's enchanting debut.

"Sometimes the student becomes the teacher, lad. Thank you. But be alert now, for the owner of the amulet can't be far away."

Laegaire then puts a finger to his lips. He waves

the group of two wounded, two children, and Morici behind a row of oaks with some thick gorse for cover. Laegaire heads to the other side of the clearing with the abbesses. We all cluster around the protection of the oaks. I grab the one nearest me. I hear an unexpected giggle. Then the oak blinks at me. This calms me during turmoil. A voice whispers in my ear, "Trust your heart. Trust in the power of enchantment no matter what happens." The voice reminds me of Ankara. I also remember how Morici struck him down with her powers. I sense a similar peril upon us. I wonder if we can trust Morici as an ally. "Trust her." The whispering voice is Gabrielle's. I grab Morici's hand and stare into her eyes.

"I trust you to help us." I see a tear form in the corner of her eye. Her face softens amidst this attack of hawks and the threat of foes.

"Thanks, Deidre." She holds my hand tightly and pulls me into a hug. "I will defend you and your friends. My allegiance is to the Tuatha and your family. You are the rightful heirs of the throne." I squeeze her arm in reassurance.

The crunching of brush by heavy feet ends our whispers. All eyes rivet toward the sound. I see their white crust, thick and heavy, more ice than men, these guards of Brugh Donn. Their eyes are only slits. The weight of their ice-armored bodies makes their steps shake the earth like elephants. They are large, so large. I shiver and hold Morici's hand. Despite the cold morning breeze, sweat beads on my forehead.

"Draw your sword, Deidre. You may need it." Then this woman transforms into the most beautiful black raven before my eyes. The raven rests on my arm, winks at me, and flies off. I see her effortlessly dodge a hawk. Her two wounded friends take after her and fly at the icy behemoths. Their squeals are like the call of bagpipes to battle. But I am alone and not very sure of myself. I take in a deep breath and move closer to the others.

Both abbesses, Brigit and Margaret, stand tall with drawn swords, waving them like wings above their heads. They rush into the attackers, knocking away swords as though flicking flies. Laegaire smiles at their battle acumen for a moment before assisting them. I feel emboldened, but nervous.

A sword falls inches in front of my eyes. I pull back and fall to the ground. An icy giant three times the size of Laegaire prepares for another swing. A battle cry erupts next to me. Culain cuts the guard's sword in two as though it is made of wax. He slashes at his armor and shatters the breastplate. Ice explodes everywhere. The frame inside the ice looks weak and frail. The man turns to run like a cornered mouse. Culain grabs my hand and helps me off the ground. His smile gives me strength.

More men appear quickly, dozens of them. I surprise myself as I squeal a war cry of my own, and charge two of them, unafraid. I trip over the broken sword and fall spread-eagle to the ground. Culain rushes in front of me with a speed I had only seen before in Lugh. His sword moves like a sickle, reaping a harvest of broken swords, broken armor, and broken ice. I feel the ice melting on me and watch it steam from my sword. The sword lifts me up and I move suddenly as though I too am as swift as light.

Without a drop of blood spilled, the icy marauders pound a fast path back toward Doe Castle. I think I am becoming quite the warrior as I brandish my sword in victory. I feel flush with confidence.

Then I notice the darkening sky. The winds rise to a squall. The crows are forced to land. I see the oaks straining against the wind. I remember Ankara's fall. I look for Morgar.

The first lightning bolt knocks me to the ground. The force hurls my sword to the base of oaks and knocks breath out of me. Sweat drips from my forehead and my heart pounds. As the flash fades, I see Morici in front of me. Has she hurled bolts again? Her face is focused across the field toward the glitter of ice that shimmers at its edge. I see the head, resembling Morici, but with darker features, more aged in callousness. The laugh is the same as at Emerald Mountain.

"Ye simple fools! How dare ye challenge Morgar?"

Another bolt of lightning appears and strikes a limb of oak. I feel its pain and hear its cry. I run for my sword, but another bolt knocks it away.

"You, Morgar, are the fool." Morici stands tall, iceless, but with the rising fire of love for us. But I also see the ice on her heart center. I feel her rising hatred of her father and his dark deeds, for leading her down such a black and barren path. The next lightning bolt comes from her. It strikes Morgar directly, disengaging huge chunks of ice. Much like at Emerald Mountain, Morgar cannot move. There is too much enchantment here coming from the abbesses, Morici, Laegaire, Culain, and, yes, from me. I see a flicker of doubt rise in the small slits opened to his eyes.

"These tricks of yers are no match for me, Morici. Remember, I taught ye everything ye know." He directs a hawk to a dive at Morici. A bolt of lightning emerges from her eyes and stuns the hawk. It squeals and flies away.

"I have tricks of my own, father, of which you do not understand."

Another bolt from Morici explodes enough of the ice by Morgar's feet to allow him to move. The iciness still in her heart is altering her aim. Morgar slips from view. I feel a renewed passion for Morici, wondering why I doubted her. The sweat on my brow has dried to a salty cake around my lips. I lick them as my eyes scan the field.

Morici rushes swiftly in Morgar's direction. Culain is at her side. Morgar's lightning strikes the oak next to them. I hear the groan of Ankara from the falling oak. It warns them.

"Move quickly, my children." I pray that they hear.

The deft speed they use to avoid the falling branches amazes me. Morgar appears again, with new agility. Morici is seething now. My heart goes out to her. She is yielding to the same darkness of hatred that she has been escaping. She creates a multitude of flashes with brilliant bolts of light, but each one succeeds only in making Morgar more mobile by removing his protective ice from around his legs.

Culain charges with his sword as Morgar evades Morici's strikes. His sword strike knocks Morgar to the ground with a thundering jolt. Yet the ice remains intact.

Morgar uses the roundness of the ice to roll away down the slope. Morici follows with strikes of continued intensity, but I see the ice growing on her chest. I see the venom in her eyes. Her strikes keep missing. As Morgar reaches the bottom of the slope, he fells an oak near my friends, with another groan and warning. Morici barely slips away beneath its falling branches. I clench my sword hilt, nearly expecting to hear Morici's scream. Not for now.

The abbesses have held me back as we watch in awe this battle of father and daughter. Strangely I am not afraid. But I feel a growing sadness for Morici as I see rage overtake the love that has been healing her.

Then I see them. Laegaire and Sultain. Sultain uses an oaken stick to stay on his feet. They both carry their swords as they move in Morgar's direction. They are on a rocky slope and move slowly. Morgar strikes boulders above and behind them. They struggle to avoid them. Culain charges Morgar again, but not before Morgar's lighting strike makes a direct hit to Sultain's chest that brings him to the ground, as blood spreads heavily over the blackened wound. I put my hand to my chest and almost feel the ache of the strike in me. Culain cries out in his own deep pain, a pain that weakens a blow that otherwise would be the end of Morgar. Never could there be a more powerful sword-strike. Ice flies for hundreds of yards. Morgar tumbles the length of two great oaks. The sparks and steam of the strike create a spray that sprinkles the field with glittering reflections of the sun that just popped out. The ice mist settles on our faces and arms like sleet, cold and sharp.

Culain, however, has no more interest in the tumbling Morgar. His only concern is for Sultain. He runs to him. Morici, however, sees this as her opportunity to complete a victory. She runs to the rocky hill and hurls bolts of lightning that strike at Morgar, but also at the strong oak next to him. She does not hear its squeal, nor feel its pain. She only strikes blindly, aimlessly in her rage. Morgar sees his opening. He strikes the great ancient oak standing over Morici. She cannot hear its voice as it falls.

"Flee, Morici, or I will crush you." This loving oak falls. Its weight buries Morici along with uprooted earth and stones. I bury my face in my hands, dropping my sword.

I do not know whom I feel more sadness for – Culain, whose father is bleeding to death; Morici, my friend who is crushed under the weight of a great oak; or the great oaks themselves that fall in this battle vainly warning my friends. My heart is heavy. Even as I see Morgar flee the scene, knowing that his power alone is not enough to defeat us, I know also that the source of his power, fear and anger, has penetrated our hearts again and led to this standoff.

"It's time to release the vile poison of fear and the bitterness of anger, Deidre. For everyone." I know the voice and look up and see her. Her golden locks ripple in the bright sunlight. Her wings hover over me. "Trust in your love. Love your trust."

Gabrielle strengthens me despite my sadness. Then, to my surprise, I see the raven-like wings of Nacham.

"It's time for love to defeat fear, Deidre. The power is within you."

I never thought I would hear such words from Nacham. Tears fill my eyes. I open my arms and my faeries fly to me.

I hear Ankara's voice vibrate with a whisper from all the oaks in the glen.

"Listen to them, me sweet Deidre. The power to heal dwells within ye. Trust it."

My belief grows and I trust.

I hear the sweet melody of Lugh's flute resonate in the distance as he plays his song while Culain, kneeling over his father, sheds tears

I run to him and place a healing hand upon his back. I love my friend with a well of compassion and sadness at his loss. I am grateful to be with him at his moment of need.

He hugs me, and Gabrielle, and Nacham.

Chapter 4

A Warrior Falls

 aegaire quietly glides to Sultain's side. The Enchanter gently places his hands over Sultain's weakened body. The wise one calls upon the deep powers of the realm.

"Great Oaks of the Forest, Sweet faeries of the Tuatha, Ancestors of Eire, we call upon your healing grace." His prayers are quiet but with resonant conviction and his eyelids hold firmly closed.

Culain continues to cry, knowing his father's life is at the edge. I put my arm around him and share my tears.

Sultain opens his eyes and weakly reaches out his

hand for Culain's. Their hands touch softly, but firmly, as Sultain considers the face of his son.

"Ye have the gift. Use it well, me son." He coughs, struggling with breath.

"Da, I will." Culain buries his head on Sultain's shoulder as he continues to squeeze his hand. Leagaire imparts healing energy to Sultain's chest with one hand and gently places the other on Culain's shoulder. The sadness about us feels like a thick, stifling fog.

Breezes rustle through the oaks. I raise my eyes to these grand tree towers of strength and listen to the echoing voices, sharing the inevitable news.

"His spirit passes to the Otherworld. He no longer dwells among men."

Winds rise around us all, bending branches and blowing loose leaves. Suddenly there is a stillness.

Culain gives his father's hand one last squeeze. Laegaire withdraws his hands and looks at Culain.

"Your brave father never gave in to the icy fears of despair. He never stopped believing in the king and queen, even when desperation overtook them. He never lost hope in his son. And, today, he lives on in you, Culain." I hold Culain tighter and he watches Laegaire silently, drawing each word into his heart before speaking to us.

"He didn't die in vain. I will see the throne returned to its rightful owners. I will defend the Tuatha, her king and queen, and…"

He turns and looks directly into my eyes.

"I will defend you, Princess Deidre, and restore you to your parents."

Not only do I believe him, but I trust without question.

"And I will support you, Culain!"

We hug and cry. Time begins to blur. We sit on a grassy knoll holding each other. The rest of our band begins to prepare a funeral pyre. They place the finest robes available upon Sultain, as suits the king's chief counsel and defender. Then the Abbess Brigit shouts with a booming voice.

"Morici's body is gone! Gone!"

Laegaire and Ermanci stride over to the huge fallen oak that appeared to crush her above tumbled stone and earth. They push back branches, roll away stones, and dig at dark earth. Blackened with peat, they finally give up.

"There are no signs of Morici, not even a piece of

cloth. It's as though she vanished. She's a shape shifter, though, maybe she escaped." Suspicion tinges Laegaire's voice. Does he think she has abandoned us, or does he think she is dead?

Ermanci looks concerned.

"Only Morici can shape-shift during daylight, but it draws all of her strength. She may be weak and wounded. I will go with me friends to find her."

Laegaire and the Abbesses do not stop him as the two injured crows follow him into the woods, but I sense uneasiness.

"If she's alive, my biggest fear is that she will try to take on Morgar again on her own. We need to stay together and deal with him as a team." Laegaire speaks words that echo the sentiment of the camp. I need to speak.

"If she's alive, she will return and help us. We can trust her." The words come out of me, but I somehow do not feel as if I am speaking. They feel planted in me. I believe in their love. I feel a tingle in my heart.

"Deidre is right. Morici may give in to anger, but she is too smart to willingly engage Morgar alone. She'll return." Culain's words are firm. His voice brings us back to the reality of his loss.

"Then let's attend to the dead." The Abbess Brigit crosses herself and heads to the funeral pyre.

The church may not approve this sacred pyre, but Abbesses Brigit and Margaret know it honors both the ancients and the spirit of the church. Sultain was a man afire with life and his pyre would be a tribute to him as his body returns to the womb of Ulster.

Culain and I gather flowers and oak branches to adorn Sultain's remains. The abbesses collect herbs to burn like incense in the fire, a pungent reminder of a great man of Eire. Laegaire keeps walking around the pyre reciting old incantations honoring Sultain's ancestors. He crosses his hands over his heart and gave thanks for Sultain's service. The nearby fallen Oaks have provided the timber to shape the rectangular bed of the pyre to give Sultain his final support.

When all is in place, Ermanci returns with his two crow friends on either shoulder.

"We find no signs of Morici nearby and it's too dangerous for us to roam alone. I will shape-shift after dark and we'll serve ye as scouts, just as we did Morici. If she returns, it will be to all of ye."

"Join us, then, Ermanci, in our funeral for Sultain." Laegaire extends a handshake of friendship.

We all gather in front of the pyre. Each of us brings one gift for Sultain to take with him in his afterlife journey. Brigit drapes an intricate handkerchief of Irish linen over his chest. Margaret places a rosary of wooden beads about his neck. Laegaire withdraws his tattered cap and puts it above the head, as his long grey hair billows into the breeze. Ermanci withdraws the bright sash he wears across his chest and lays it next to Brigit's kerchief. I take one of my two wooden pipes, carved in the Enchanted Forest, and whistle Lugh's tune as I dance around the pyre. Then I lay it gently in Sultain's hand. The weight of tears brings rivulets to my cheeks, but I wipe them away quickly with my arms. I miss him and my heart goes out to Culain.

Culain has a small sack of items. As he wipes away the tears that come, he gently removes the slain forms of Morici's crows felled by Morgar's hawks. Then he pulls out the two amulets, filled with bright new gems. He places one in Sultain's hand and one around his neck. He pulls out his flute and plays. I somehow hear the distant wailing keens in the banshee forest. I am grateful to know that the banshee faeries honor him. A brave son of Ulster defended his home with valor before crossing the veil.

After a final hug with each of us, Culain bids his father a final tribute.

"Da, I didn't get much time with you, but your heart always touched me. I know your love of Ulster, of Eire, and of the High King. I will always hold the example of your courage and loyalty in my heart. I love you, Da."

Then we all make a circle around Sultain and his wooden pyre, pull out our swords and lay them upon the dried twigs and brush underneath.

Sparks begin to flash from the tips of the swords, gently igniting the pyre, as we all step back. Darkness is falling upon the woods and the flames leap into the sky like fireflies. We all bow our heads in respect and sing ancient songs of honor.

As we withdraw to the campfire in silence, Laegaire raises his arms and speaks with a quiet certainty.

"My friends, we have lost a great leader from our midst, a loyal subject of the High King. It is time, now, to complete our funeral ritual and leave this camp. Surely, Morgar, his hawks, and the castle guard will return soon. We must find a safe refuge."

Suddenly we hear the shuffle of wings. Instinctively we lower ourselves closer to the ground.

"Fear not, me friends. I come to aid ye."

I run to Maeve. I recognize her voice instantly. Her warm smile greets me and her arms and wings envelop me. I never thought I would see the Queen of the Faeries outside the Enchanted Forest. My heart rises and I squeal with delight.

"I am sorry for yer loss, my friends. I come to join ye in engaging Morgar and Brugh Donn." Reassuring words.

The rest of our band joins in a circle around us. Culain speaks first.

"I will scout Doe castle alone, my Queen. Take the rest with you to the Ards Forest for your protection."

I protest immediately. "No! Culain, you must come with us or at least take someone with you."

Culain responds as though he knows what I am going to say. "Deidre, I know you will be safe with Maeve, Laegaire and the Abbesses. I will take Ermanci and his two friends with me. They will scout for me and keep me safe."

Ermanci shakes his head approvingly and the two crows land on Culain's shoulders. Laegaire's silence and a raised staff affirm Culain's plan.

I cannot bear to be separated from Culain again. I run to him in tears. He gently hugs me as the crows take flight.

"Deeder. I'll be okay. I have Lugh with me as

well."

Brigit comes over and persuades me to embrace her skirts. Maeve stretches her wings and speaks with a knowing heart.

"Culain speaks wisely. This Morgar is a great threat not only to Ulster, but also to the Enchantment itself. Culain and Ermanci will scout his positions and return to us as we prepare to defend ourselves."

"What about my parents?" My question hangs in the air thickly, making everyone feel heavy.

"Culain will scout for them as well. Morgar knows that if they are alive they will draw us back to him. He wants to destroy all of us."

Laegaire steps forward. His grey beard and hair make him look experienced and wise.

"Culain indeed speaks with wisdom, Deidre. The High King is best served if we follow this plan." He looks around at all in the circle. "All in favor raise your hand."

The rest raise their hands immediately. But I think of my parents, still in the clutches of Brugh Donn, Morgar, and the castle guard. Then one of the crows gently brushes against my arm. I raise it.

Everyone applauds. I do not smile. I grab up my few belongings as the rest do the same. I worry that a spark of revenge might be motivating Culain's actions, but he looks calm and determined as he talks with Ermanci and holds one of the crows on his wrist. Culain imitates the crow's squawk, just like the other birdcalls we share. Then I do smile. I trust my friend.

Sparks rise brightly as the funeral pyre still burns and the campfire embers remain red as we walk away into the dark oak woods. A final tear falls for Sultain and I glance back at Culain. Sounds and whispers of wind that once would bring me to worry, simply sound like tunes of my trusted friends, the oaks and the breeze. I feel at home, even though we have only moonlight to guide us. We wave goodbye to Culain and Ermanci and watch them move toward the castle. Seeing Culain leaving once again feels too much for me. I shout after him, run in leaps and bounds, almost knocking him over with my bear hug. He gently separates us.

"All will be well, Deeder. Trust in the Enchantment." He then turns into the forest and Abbess Bridgit gently grabs my hand and we turn back to our path as I wipe the tears away.

The journey is uphill and stony so it is not long before my legs ache and I ask for rest and sit on a rock. I close my eyelids, but before I know it, daybreak startles my eyes open. A rooster's cock-a-doodle-do chimes in the distance. I lift my head from Laegaire's shoulder. I do not know how long he has carried me, this strong old enchanter.

I rub my eyes as he lowers me to the ground. "Are we close to the Enchanted Forest?" My voice is scratchy and hoarse, but Laegaire understands me.

"We have a little change in plan." He sits me down on a mound. We stand at the same place where the abbesses had taken up camp near a small cave when Culain and I had first ventured into the Enchanted kingdom. Maeve is flying around the cave with arms waving in ceremony.

"She's placing a protection spell on the abbesses' cave. Brigit and Margaret can't enter the enchantment. They're too contaminated with the earthly world. But they'll be safe."

"I thought we were all to stay together."

"Even the best of plans must yield to change, my princess."

So, it is just Laegaire and Maeve joining my return to the Enchanted Forest. Strange. I met them both there, where they became my supporters. But eventually I was all alone with the dark queen at Emerald Mountain. Will there be another such test for me?

"Don't forget us!" How can I forget Nacham and Gabrielle? Yes, indeed, it still is a strong team. But I miss the others. Laegaire plumbs my thoughts.

"If Morici were with us, she too would have been barred from the Enchantment. After all, you defeated her at Emerald Mountain."

"No, Laegaire. I didn't defeat her. I merely helped her find herself. I encouraged her. I would speak on her behalf to gain entry to the Forest."

"But would Ankara agree?" Laegaire speaks as if Ankara is alive. Morici's lightning destroyed him. Or had it?

"I will ask him, if he recovers!" I then release any fledgling expectations of his return.

"Let's bid farewell to Brigit and Margaret." I nod agreement as I look about me and feel the warm presence of trees, flowers, and grass supporting me. As we walk arm-in-arm, a small, quiet voice whispers – a familiar voice. I raise my hand to the others for stillness. The endearing voice speaks with urgency.

"Hurry, Deidre! We need ye right away."

Ankara's voice is unmistakable – distant, concerned, demanding.

"Ankara calls us." Maeve's voice speaks before I

can. Her furrowed brow belies an emerging concern. The tone and the reaction the Queen Faerie dampen my rising joy over hearing Ankara's voice.

Silently Maeve motions to Laegaire to pick me up again. She swoops down and lifts both of us and we fly in the direction of Ankara's voice. The abbesses wave goodbye with strained looks as they retreat to the cave.

We fly over the Bend, where the dark riders accosted us in the Abbess' carriage. I remember the spill. A dark opening in the floor of the woods draws our attention. The veiled passage is small, but wide enough for Maeve to fly right through it.

The darkness blinds me. I feel Laegaire hold me tight. The speed of flight, almost like the initial fall, feels like a windstorm. A voice rings out.

"Deidre, come, now!"

Although her lips are hidden from view, I hear the great Queen Maeve respond.

"We're on our way, Ankara."

Chapter 5

Darkness Invades

 aegaire and Maeve almost suffocate me between them, but their grip feels secure and safe in flight. The darkness of this mysterious cavern entry to the Enchantment presses in on me. I see only the faint glow in the eyes of my companions. But my heart senses something more, a rising urgency behind their eyes. Impenetrable walls of blackness imprison my spirit. This transition between worlds disorients me. My head spins, but I refuse to pass out. I resist an urge to break free from Laegaire's strong arms.

As we emerge, brilliant light flashes like lightning. My eyes close tight by instinct, but brightness still penetrates my eyelids, right to the back of my head. Wind rushes as Laegaire sets me down upon a greenish mound. I gingerly open my eyes and glare washes across my vision. My breath sucks into me like a filling bagpipe. I had forgotten the beauty of this place -- the greener greens, the bluer blues, the greater depth of perception. It overwhelms me in a reassuring way. I feel lighter, more whimsical, faerie-like.

"Greetings, me queen, me princess, and me liege."

I cannot believe the image speaking before us. There stands Ankara! Even taller and larger than when we first met. How can this be? Ankara answers my thoughts.

"Me dear Deidre, it warms me heart to see ye again. As ye can see, the power of enchantment has restored me. Time here is not like it is in your world. Things change more quickly."

Before I respond, Laegaire steps forward.

"You said we were needed right away, Ankara. Speak up, Great Oak."

Queen Maeve flies over and rests upon Ankara's largest branch. I circle my arms around his trunk. Laegaire, however, is not so touched by this re-union. His hands are on his hips and he stares at Ankara with a severe look.

"Me friends, Darkness has entered the Enchantment."

"Be specific, Great Oak. What Darkness?" Laegaire sounds impatient. I can see a rising concern on Maeve's face as she flies to Laegaire's side. I just hold Ankara tighter.

"Morgar has breached the Sand Castle."

We all suck in our breaths. Maeve's furrowed frown tells me that this Queen of the Enchantment cannot imagine such a breach without her knowledge.

"This Morgar is clever. He shape-shifted into a hawk and scattered a thin film of pirated faerie dust along the way to lull us all to sleepiness. Before we knew, his whole host of hawks had captured the faeries and leprechauns and held the castle hostage."

I grip my face with fright. My good friends who taught me the way of the faerie are in danger!

"We must release them and reclaim the castle!" I brandish my sword with strong resolve.

Laegaire puts a hand to my wrist.

"Not so fast, Deidre." He looks at Maeve and back at Ankara.

"You have more to tell us, don't you, Ankara?"

Sinister hawks hover in the distance. I don't know if one of them has spotted us yet.

"Morgar knows that Culain is not with ye, that the Abbesses and Morici are not with ye. Without them, ye are no match for him, even with Maeve."

"This can't be true; this is Maeve's kingdom!" I assert the need to free the faeries and leprechauns in the castle. Maeve looks at me with compassion.

"Deidre, this kingdom belongs to all of us. I only rule it with the support of all the loving beings. Morgar has dulled their senses." I put away my sword. Laegaire comes over and puts his arm on my shoulder, bending his knees so that his face is at my level.

"The Enchantment also needs the support of the world of men and women, especially those of Ulster and Eire. But they too have hardened hearts, falling into despair and the rule of fear."

I push away his arm and pull out my sword.

"I am the Princess of Ulster and my heart is free and strong. I will use the sword of Lugh to defeat Morgar."

Laegaire smiles kindly at me.

"Indeed, my princess, your support is alive and vigorous. So is Culain's. So are the hearts of the abbesses and many in the Resistance. But the three of us here are not ready to engage Morgar – not yet." He winks at me.

hand. A branch of the Oak knocks the sword from my

"Listen, child, to me liege, the Great Enchanter Laegaire. His wisdom and mine sing the same song. Be patient. Gather in Culain, Morici, and the abbesses before ye return to Emerald Mountain."

I shiver at the mention of Emerald Mountain.

"Yes, Deidre, ye met Morici's challenge on yer own, but yer next test is to call upon yer allies to meet the challenge of Morgar."

Laegaire looks puzzled. "I thought Morgar was at the Enchanted Castle."

"Yes, me liege, but ye must engage him at Emerald Mountain. Let his hawks find ye there. Ye must draw him away from the Sand Castle and the faeries."

This makes sense to me, but another question demands expression.

"Can the abbesses join us?"

"Yes!" Both the voices of Ankara and Maeve ring out in unison. "Now that Morgar has breached our gates, all supporters of enchantment are welcome."

Ankara adds: "Now be off with ye three!"

Hawks swoop down toward us. I draw out my sword, but to no avail. Ankara's longest branch thrashes the hawk enough to knock him to the ground with feathers flying. The squawking bird quickly regains its composure and flies away.

"Like I said, be off with ye!"

We get it. Laegaire scoops me up and Maeve flies over to embrace us both in flight. I wave to Ankara. One day, I hope, I will spend some time with him without imminent danger. I pray this will come to be. I sigh as he disappears and we approach the veil between the Enchantment and Eire.

This time I just close my eyes and breathe deeply as I place my trust in Laegaire's arms and Maeve's wings. My wisdom tells me to trust theirs. The fate of the Enchanted Forest itself rests with us. My impulsive desire to engage Morgar must simply simmer.

When we emerge to the other side, light looks weak and colors bland. How sad that Eire's countryside cannot know its full beauty. I sigh a little and begin to search for abbesses. Then I see him – a dark flier, a familiar messenger, a black crow. He flies in front of us. The bird speaks.

"Greetings, travelers!" The Spanish accent of Ermanci makes me giggle. Then a second bird lands on my shoulder.

"Good to see ye, sweet Deidre." My heart rises at Morici's voice. She's alive! I reach to pat her head, but she flies off and calls Maeve and Ermanci.

"Follow me. Culain awaits us at the cave."

We spot him searching the area. No sign of either abbess. As we land, I run to Culain and give him a bear hug. His quick smile assures me of his joy in seeing us, but it fades quickly.

"They have captured the Abbesses!"

"Morgar?"

"No, the church of Patrick." I gasp and cover my open mouth with both hands.

"But the abbesses care for the poor there and lead the church's abbeys. Why would those good people capture them?"

"Not only have we aroused a Resistance, but Brugh Donn, in turn, has made alliances with the Bishop. He sends them gold and he foments the parishes against the abbesses. He calls them pagan witches."

This lie boils hot inside me. How dare they?

"Why does he call them witches?"

"Because they consort with faeries. Because they have captured the Princess Deidre."

I pull my sword and brandish it over my head.

"Do I look like a prisoner?" My emotions cloud my thoughts.

"Calm down, Deeder, we all know these confused parishioners are misled by the spells of Morgar and a web of lies. But the priests and people see the abbesses as evil."

Morici flies in front of us, landing on my sword.

"Deidre, my father is clever with lies, just as I used to be. I have learned from my folly, but the flock follows its leaders even down dark paths. I'm sorry to have been such a leader, but I know the power of lies."

"Yes, Morici, I know. But Morgar now controls the Enchanted Castle! Ankara just told us and sent us back to get you, Culain and the abbesses."

The news stuns Morici. She spontaneously transforms into human form with a fury in her eyes that I had not seen since our Emerald Mountain duel.

"I knew we could not underestimate him!"

I nod in agreement and give her a hug. She pushes me away with a stern look, but the fire has melted to an intense focus as she speaks.

"Ankara is right, Deidre. When my father escaped us in our first battle, I learned that my own emotions hardened my heart and weakened me. We need each other. None of us can go it alone. We must unite our powers."

Morici's words surprise me. She has released the grip of her resentment toward her father. In its place is a resolve to make amends and free the Enchantment from Morgar's grip. Love, not fear and anger, will save the Tuatha faeries.

Morici shape shifts back to bird-form and lands on Culain's arm. Ermanci already sits upon Culain's shoulder. My friend walks to the top of a mound, raises his arms and addresses us.

"We must be of one mind! I have met with Lugh himself. He tells us we must go to the village, to the church of St. Michael the Archangel. We first must break the spell of darkness and deceit that has been cast upon the parishioners before returning to the Enchanted Forest."

Laegaire raises his staff. "The pupil now leads us. Follow him." I sense both pride and a tinge of regret in sharing leadership.

Chapter 6

St. Michael the Archangel

 s worry swirls in my mind about the faeries and leprechauns back in the forest, my feet still stay lockstep behind Culain and Laegaire. *The abbesses are gone, yes, but I see Maeve fly overhead and relish her warble to me. Hooves thunder nearby. The familiar whinnies of Brigit's horses announce their return to our service. Laegaire lifts me up on the tallest mount. Culain climbs the other. The rest fly ahead of us. The echoes of galloping steeds reverberate through the forest. I have no idea how we will sway the minds of the parishioners. A voice, meant just for me, does!*

"Trust in yourself, Deidre. Trust your friends. Trust the power of enchantment."

Nacham and Gabrielle whisper in rare, but clear, unison, one in each ear!

"Listen to Lugh. Trust, too, in him."

I experience a warmth in my heart that calms me amidst the pounding hooves of my black stallion. My old thoughts still entreat me to be afraid and to doubt, but trust is overcoming them.

As we approach St. Michael's, I notice Morgar's feathered sentinels on the spire, in the belfry and in the high branches around the church. Icy stares of dark-eyed hawks almost cut through us as we approach, but I sense that they only serve as eyes and ears of Morgar here. They will be passive for now.

A throng of animated parishioners stands in front of the church next to a cluster of Celtic crosses in the cemetery. Their faces quickly turn toward us as our steeds' clamor rises.

Caleb stands in front of the crowd, the same Caleb who pretended to be my father. His balding head and wide waist are unmistakable. His dour and hostile face glares at us. And beside him? Yes. Martha in clackety shoes and a showy red skirt! Her furrowed brow rises when she sees me.

I try to pull Laegaire's cape around me. I want to

be gone from this place. Had I not run away from these people? My heart begins to waver. I remember the bruises on my backside and the blood upon my lips. Somehow, even Morgar feels less threatening than these caretakers who abused me for so many years. Then I see Abbess Brigit. Caleb notices my recognition and strikes her with a blow across the face that knocks her to the ground. Had the other villagers not held her back, I am sure Caleb would be eating dirt.

Nacham speaks first. "This is not the time to shy away, Deidre. Now is the time of truth. Listen to your heart."

"Show them who you are!" Gabrielle flies in front of me. She points to the ice forming over my heart.

"Melt it away."

As I look again at the villagers, each has copious sheets of ice upon them. I had not seen it at first, but my own iciness had blinded me.

I place my hand upon my heart. "Guide me, Lugh." I jump off the horse and rush to help the Abbess to her feet. I can feel bits of ice crunch under my feet as they fall from my chest.

Caleb and Martha grab at me as the other villagers tighten their hold on the arms of the Abbess. Culain also rushes forward, but the crowd throttles him. Neither of us have drawn swords at these villagers. I see Culain's "parents" from the apothecary, Eldonna and Eamonn. They pretend not to see him. Laegaire remains on his horse. As some of the villagers approach the steed rises and kicks. Laegaire raises his staff.

"Listen, all you parishioners of St. Michael's. You may remember me. I am Laegaire, the Court Enchanter of the High King Conchubar."

Someone throws an apple at him.

"Ye're just a sorcerer of the old pagan religion, like these abbesses."

"I am the king's counselor. He's in danger."

"Lies from a druid! Ye have no power here in the presence of God and his Savior."

"My power comes from the same God and the same Savior!"

This hushes the crowd. No one ever uttered such claims before. The power of the church of Patrick from the same source as the power of the Celtic druids? It sounds inconceivable. In my heart, I trust in its truth, but these villagers are in no mood to agree.

The parish priest, Father Malachy, steps forward. He is a strong, tall man, who I had seen at the abbey many times — friendlier times.

"How dare ye blaspheme in front of the church of the Archangel?"

Laegaire dismounts and holds his staff upward.

"You may challenge me, but can you challenge the daughter of the High King himself?"

Again, a hush. Then a grumble rolls through the crowd.

Caleb calls out. "She's dead!"

"I am right here, Caleb, and you know it!" I give him a swift kick to the shin and throw dust into Martha's face and she lets me go. I run in front of Laegaire.

"Laegaire speaks the truth. I am Deidre, of the house of Conall, daughter of King Conchubar."

This time the apple hits me squarely on the shoulder. "Liar! Ye're just the little brat of Caleb and Martha."

Then Brigit, blood trickling from her lip, speaks with authority. "Tell them, Caleb, about our arrangement."

Caleb backs off, temporarily speechless. Martha steps forward.

"We took care of the orphan girl for the abbess for

just a few pennies a week. The ingrate! Putting on the airs of royalty! Who does she think she is, the little wench?" The words fire up the villagers, who start to move towards me. Then I see the black birds -- Morici, Ermanci, and two of their black-feathered companions. They come screaming down in between us. The crowd backs off, except for Martha.

"See, the wench herself is just a little witch. She calls upon the darkness of the crows." The crowd agrees with her, but gets a little edgy that I might have power.

I wait to see if the hawks would participate, but they stand their ground, knowing that their involvement would give the impression that Laegaire and I have some additional powers. But Martha is undaunted by the crows and comes to grab me. Laegaire stretches forth his staff to block her path.

"Out of me way, old man." As she starts to push against his staff, a short red-bearded man steps boldly in front of her.

"As I am Colin McGee, I call ye both liars, Martha and Caleb!" Martha backs off and my friend Colin launches up the cobblestone church steps to speak to the throng.

"This girl tells the truth. Caleb himself told me he got five shillings a week to take care of this daughter of

King Conchubar. He was supposed to keep it a secret, but he told me."

"Quiet ye cauldron-maker. Pagan!" Caleb moves to strike the little man, but Father Malachy holds him back.

"What else did he say, McGee?"

"He said that a messenger of the Dark Queen, Morici, had come asking for the princess, and offered a bag of gold crowns for information." The crowd grumbles with doubts. Caleb rushes toward Colin with his hand raised to strike. Martha grabs Caleb and slaps him in the face.

"Ye never told me about the gold crowns, ye lout!" Martha realizes her mistake. The crowd circles Martha with rising suspicion and disgust. Colin speaks one last time.

"Parishioners of St. Michael's. This young girl, in your very midst, is Princess Deidre of Conall, daughter of the High King. Abbess Brigit was entrusted with her care by this man, Laegaire." I run to Colin and hug him. Some of the parishioners begin to clap, but Fr. Malachy raises his hand for silence.

"Is there anyone else who can vouch for this Deidre, to prove that she is not a daughter of darkness?"

A frail, old woman hobbles forward. She is the hag, the same old woman who helped me escape the Inn and showed me kindness.

"Who be ye?" demands one of the parishioners.

"Just a poor old woman who needed some stew. This little missy took pity on a stranger like me."

"Does that make her a princess?" Fr. Malachy does not sound impressed.

"No, but Martha here still has her royal necklace." Martha's face reddens as the hag points to her neck with her cane.

"She lies!"

Fr. Malachy walks over to Martha. The edge of a chain was visible about her neck.

"Show us what's on that chain?" The pastor's voice is stern.

Caleb shouts, "Don't let them see it."

Despite her protests, Malachy lifts the chain and finds that it holds the bright gold medallion clearly embossed with the crest of the High King Conchubar himself.

"Martha, where did ye get this necklace?"

"I got the necklace from the Abbess, but Caleb

never told me about the gold. Ye lout!" She struggles to strike her husband.

The crowd is beginning to believe us when Caleb starts up again.

"Ask the Abbess. She made up the whole story. This little wench is no more royalty than ye or me. The Abbess is a pagan who talks to faeries. She's just a witch!"

This strikes fear in the crowd and grumbling renews. The hag steps forward again and pounds her walking stick upon a stone.

"Nonsense! This man just wants to protect his hide. What was the last time ye even saw him in yer church? I know these abbesses. Yes, they still value the spirit of the Old Religion, but they are not at all against the New. Let go of yer bigotry."

I look at the fire in her eyes and suddenly I remember something this old woman said when I met her. I need to ask her again.

"Old woman, what's your name?"

She looks kindly in my direction and speaks softly.

"I told ye before, missy. Me name is Maeve." She has shape-shifted into the old hag again to help me, just as she did that day at the Inn. My heart goes out to her, but

I know to keep my feelings in check.

The throng is turning ugly. All this talk of pagans and spells and faeries is beginning to strike fear in the hearts of these simple folk. Fr. Malachy has taught them to fear pagan ideas and to let go of their old myths about faeries and the Tuatha. Many of them, however, hold on to their simple faith in the forest creatures and the message of the one God, the same God of the Old and the New religions. Different rituals. Different paths. But the same loving God!

Laegaire raises his staff to the grousing crowd.

"Fr. Malachy, I suggest that you take Deidre into the church alone and speak with her and with your God to determine whether she speaks the truth." Fr. Malachy looks a little uneasy with accepting the burden of finding the truth. His uncertainty shows in his frown. Especially since his superiors were so sure that the abbesses were heretics and witches. Culain breaks away from those holding him and runs in front of the priest.

"My father, Sultain, the Defender of the King, now lies dead, due to the same lies. The king and queen need their daughter now. Please listen to Laegaire." Fr. Malachy steps back, more than a wee bit astonished. Is this boy the same quiet bird-caller and street-urchin? He is even more confused, but the boy's intensity persuades him.

"So be it. Deidre, come with me. No one else!"

As the Red Sea opened for Moses, so does a path part for me. St. Michael the Archangel church is a simple village church, but the doors are heavy. The smell of incense and musty food offerings linger in the air. Some young men pull open the doors for us to enter. I feel isolated, but somehow comforted by Fr. Malachy. His tone is firm, but gentle. The arched ceilings are dark, but light pours through the stained-glass windows facing the sun. I look up at the image of St. Michael, sword in hand, defeating the figure of the prince of darkness. The face of Michael the Archangel looks strangely familiar, but the thought quickly leaves me as the priest sets me upon a bench by the altar. Above the altar stands a statue of St. Michael in much the same pose as in the stained glass.

"Deidre, what's going on here? Has the abbess put these silly ideas into yer head — all this nonsense about faeries and ye being a princess?"

I am uneasy with Fr. Malachy. I know the entire Enchantment is depending on me to help free us to engage Morgar, but how can I convince this staunch priest of the church? I listen to the words repeating in my heart. "Trust, trust, trust."

I take a deep breath and let the words flow.

"Father, the Abbess never told me anything about being a princess."

"What? Then what makes ye claim it?" I can tell he is getting exasperated as he paces up and down beside me, playing with the beads hanging from his waist.

"I ran away, Father. I just knew Caleb and Martha were not my real parents."

"Well, yes me dear girl, but that does not make ye daughter of a king."

"The Abbess knew all along but she kept it a secret—even to me -- so no one would tell the Dark Queen, Morici."

"Come now, girl, Morici is merely the counselor of good Brugh Donn, who rules now that Conchubar and Macha have become infirm."

"You're right, Father. She no longer is a dark queen, but it is because she has transformed. And I helped her."

"Balderdash, girl! Where do ye get such ideas? From these abbesses? They should be ashamed."

Wings flutter with a gentle rush of air, but when I turn Morici stands there in all her courtly robes. When Father catches her eyes, he pulls back, startled.

"St. Michael, defend and protect us!" His face looks a little ashen. "How did ye get in here?"

"It matters not, good Father. But St. Michael is defending and protecting your flock this moment. He sends me to let you know that Deidre speaks the truth, as do the abbesses. They love Michael and God just as you do." Fortunately, Fr. Malachy recognizes Morici. She is saving me again! I feel proud of her, but I can see the fear and doubts in Father's eyes.

"Father, did you know that St. Michael has a brother?"

Morici's question further flusters the good pastor, as he shakes his head no. I must admit myself that this is an odd question. I shake my head as well.

"My new friend Culain, whose father Sultain died yesterday in defense of the kingdom, taught me the name of Michael's brother."

Fr. Malachy and I both look at each other quizzically.

"His brother is Lugh of the Light." I hear the flute playing in the distance. I glance up at the stained-glass image of St. Michael. Yes, I think, that is why he looks so familiar. I smile and feel reassured, but when I look at the priest, I see the deep trouble in his face.

"This Lugh is just a Celtic myth, a story, like the faeries." Father is not prepared for this revelation, but I am. Why did I not see it before?

"Father, I know you are skeptical. Why not ask the patron of your church to give you a sign, so that you might discern the truth?"

"What kind of sign?"

"Why not leave that up to Michael?"

The priest paces back and forth and finally he kneels before the altar and the statue of St. Michael. He prays aloud.

"I do not pretend to understand these strange ideas that this girl and Morici present to me, Michael the Archangel, but I do not doubt ye, patron of this parish. Ye have answered me prayers many times over these 33 years as a canon of this church. Give me some clear-cut sign if this girl truly is the daughter of the high king."

Just then the light shining through the stained glass illumines the statue of Michael. Although the move is slight, the arm and sword of Michael rise higher, and a faint wind rises from nowhere and blows in the canon's face, brushing back his hair.

Morici and I cannot hear it, but Father has heard a voice. He no longer looks confused or anxious. He turns to us.

He bows to me. "Me princess, how may I best serve the crown?"

I run up to him and hug him, while Morici stands by with a smile on her face.

Then I hear the church door screech open.

"How did ye get in here, sorceress?" The harsh voice echoes those of others behind him.

"How dare ye desecrate our church!"

Chapter 7

Unconscious

he villagers surge through the door, drawn in by the sound Morici's voice and led by the growling inward rush of a big-boned brawler, sporting a wild shock of red hair, snarling for a fight. New farmer? No! I sense and envision the feathers — this is a shape-shifted hawk! The villagers, oblivious to the sham, fall in line behind this bear of a man, egging him to speak.

"How did this pagan Morici get in our church? What spell does she cast?" The throng holds behind him, almost quivering upon seeing Morici and fearing her dark power. Her legendary stories of dark magic have frightened these peaceful villagers into abandoning any of their ties to the old natural religion in favor of the Christianity of Patrick. Fr. Malachy, I could see, is not easily swayed by legends or towering men.

"This girl speaks the truth. St. Michael himself has sent me a sign!"

The oak of a farmer, however, charges like a bull, and viciously swings his staff at Morici. His scowl can curdle milk.

While my heart pounds, I cannot stop myself from rushing in front of Morici to protect her with raised hands.

"Stop! She supports King Conchu...."

I feel the rude rush of air as the whipping rod strikes me full force in the forehead, barely deflected by my arms. The light suddenly turns yellow with lightning streaks of white. I know that I am unconscious, but, instead, I feel airy and awake, like I am floating on water. I rise with an air current and watch the still form of my crumpled body on the floor with blood oozing from its head wound. Instinctively I put my hand to my forehead, but it is dry – and I wonder how I am in two places at once. My thoughts turn to the flash of an electrical bolt from Morici's hand to the redheaded hawk-man who crashes on top of my limp body. His staff clatters with a drum roll to the church's oak floor. The crowd surges around our motionless bodies. "Get him off me!" I shout unheard. When they see my body compressed like a pretzel beneath the marauder, they roll him off with shrieks. I see no breath rise from my chest. Am I dead?

Fr. Malachy bellows a shout.

"Get out of the way. Give the princess some air!" He blesses me, the me who lies below me.

"Release the others. Bring me Laegaire!"

As I scan the church, I see Laegaire float above the crowd. He smiles.

"All will be well, Deidre. You'll return to your body. You've got too much work yet to do. Trust your friends."

I look down. Brigit and Margaret circle my form like mother hens. Brigit places green balm upon my forehead. Margaret grounds my feet and pulls me back into my body. I resist as I begin to feel the rush of a sledgehammer pounding on my forehead. I blink my eyes open and my chest takes in air as I quiver in pain. The crowd cheers. I see Laegaire, the worldly one, smile into my aching eyes. Fr. Malachy's voice rings out: "Thanks be to God!" I wish I could still be floating above the fray. I drop hazily into a deep, silent unconsciousness.

While I do not see it, Culain rushes to my side. He

feels that he has failed me, as he failed Sultain. He sees that the hawk-man is gone, vanished. He knows time is short to defeat Morgar, yet his heart aches for me. I feel his love even in my unconsciousness.

He kisses my forehead. I feel it, even amid buzzing darkness and numbing pain. I float to a shadowy place where I somehow listen to Culain narrate to me what is happening outside me, even as I languish in unconsciousness:

Deidre, as I see your life ebbing away from me, I feel alone, abandoned. I still grieve the loss of my Da. I feel a burning desire to attain what both of you and he desired –- to return the rightful high king to the throne. I send a prayer to each of the twin spirits, the Archangel Michael and Lugh. I feel my heart pound with life. As I kiss your forehead and stand up, a beam of light gleams so brightly that I cover my eyes. I hear the piper. Michael's sword flashes in the stained glass. A voice rings from the blade.

"It's time to move quickly, Culain. Morgar's hawks are flying to him now. Trust Deidre with Fr. Malachy. She'll be safe here for now. Gather the warriors of light!"

Clear instructions. I feel Laegaire's eyes penetrate me with zeal. He raises his staff and speaks to the parishioners in the church.

"I promise you that dear Princess Deidre will recover, my friends, but the church and all Ulster are at risk. Brugh Donn's new Court Enchanter Morgar now threatens the kingdom with a shadow of darkness and destruction. Please, go to your homes and pray for our Resistance as we leave to confront this grave danger to all of us." The crowd has grown quiet and a bit spellbound at the resonance of his magical voice.

As the abbesses attend to you, Deidre, and I hold your hand, Father Malachy quiets the remaining doubters.

"Me good parishioners, St. Michael himself has made it clear to me that Laegaire speaks the truth, that our own lovely Deidre is indeed our courageous princess, and that we must listen to the wisdom of King Conchubar's Court Enchanter. Please, Laegaire, tell us who these brave members of your band are before ye leave on your mission to confront Morgar."

One by one, he introduces us.

"My good villagers, you know the good Abbess Brigit. A great woman of the church, she has been the protector of the princess ever since Deidre was at the Inn. She was sworn to secrecy to protect Deidre from the deadly reach of Brugh Donn." Brigit almost ignores the commendation as she pushes the crowd away from your caregivers.

A few grumbles stir, mostly from the direction of Martha and Caleb. I see their whispers and glares. "Betrayer of the church!" shouts an unknown voice.

The Abbess Brigit speaks.

"My fellow Ulstermen, release your childish fears. We all are warriors of light; only many of you do not yet know it. Open your hearts a little today, or Brugh Donn and Morgar will control your souls."

A grizzled old man with a cane, arches up his back.

"Brigit, Conchubar told us the same story years ago! Now he rots in prison and grows old like me. Yer hopes are fantasy."

"No, good brother, it is your fears that are illusion. You can choose to embrace fear or love. All warriors of light have that choice. Choose love and join us. Give us your support and prayers."

Brigit stands firm and tall, rooted in mother earth with the strength of the oaks. Her words melt some of their icy exteriors and "amens" rise on the lips of many. Laegaire hushes the crowds with raised hands like the wings of an eagle.

"Heed the fine Abbess and your good pastor. They speak the truth, the most powerful commodity in any kingdom. As the Court Enchanter of the High King, I present you the other defenders of the royal family."

Abbess Margaret attends to you, Deidre, chanting prayers and adding balm to your wound. Laegaire mentions her name, but she does not stray from her task. I am glad that the villagers are accepting us, but I grow impatient with Laegaire's introductions.

I turn to Morici and Laegaire speaks.

"Princess Deidre herself touched the

heart of Morici, the former court enchanter of Brugh Donn, and now a co-enchanter with me. Morici now is our ally and our friend. She is for us, not against us."

Gasps and murmurs filter through the crowd. Skepticism is tangible. Morici ignores both the tribute and the doubts and keeps her eyes of compassion upon you, Deidre. I see the tenderness in her soul that only you could see. You drew love out of this once embittered woman. The spark now glows in her. I am proud to have her as a friend.

Ermanci flies down on the ground around you, Deidre, chirping a healing song. Laegaire thinks of explaining him, but knows this crowd has had enough of magic today. Shape-shifting crows is a topic for another day!

I start to pace. I know that Laegaire heard Michael and Lugh's clear instructions.

"My liege, Laegaire, let us tarry no longer." Laegaire winces a little, but his countenance bears only patient tolerance.

"My friends, this is no mere boy. This is Culain, the one foretold to save Eire. His father

Sultain is only recently fallen while protecting the princess. He will lead us in saving the king.

"Culain, you are a great and mighty light warrior, but even the greatest need the support and prayers of the people of Ulster. That is why I tarry, my beloved Culain. We must entreat them to know and support our cause with their prayers." I know the wisdom in his voice, but I continue to pace. Your motionless image on the floor haunts me, as does the memory of my father. I breathe deeply and look at St. Michael's granite statue.

I doubt if anyone else sees it, but the great warrior of light arises in full array, wings spread wide. He considers my eyes and speaks wordlessly.

"Patience, young warrior. Heed Laegaire's wisdom."

Then Laegaire points to the hag.

"This old woman has stood watching over all of you for years, mostly hidden in the great Ards forest."

A villager interrupts. "This ugly hag is a curse to the village." Maeve turns to him.

"I remember ye, Brian, when ye were a lad in the woods. Ye came and watched the faeries with me. Ye sang with them when ye were alone. Ye still do! I remember yer father caught that great goose ye wanted for Christmas dinner."

The older man steps back. I see the fear in his eyes.

"She lies. I saw no faeries." His grown daughter approaches him and holds his hand.

"Da, how many times have ye told us the story of how ye asked the faeries for a goose for Christmas dinner when ye were just nine." Brian covers his eyes.

Maeve pats him on the back.

"It's alright, Brian. I will watch over ye always whether ye trust in the Enchantment or not. We love all of ye in Ulster." She turns to the crowd. "If any of ye can find even the smallest place in yer hearts to acknowledge the love and enchantment of the Ards Forest, then support us in our quest to restore the high king."

Maeve's voice is firm but gentle. She does

not demand their belief and support, but extends hers to them.

Laegaire does not introduce him, but Colin McGee steps forward.

"I am Colin McGee, the itinerant cauldron maker to ye, but I live in the Ards Forest as well. Me friends, the faeries and the leprechauns, are in great danger. On behalf of me friends who have supported this village for years, please listen to Maeve and Laegaire. Join us in meeting the present danger from the new Court Enchanter Morgar."

"How do we help?" Several women from the crowd fetch water and fresh cloths for your forehead, Deeder. Men grab you a pillow and a blanket. Their desire to help shows. Laegaire is right. We need to let them help. I breathe deeply knowing that I need to trust his wisdom more than my impulses. I need to assist Laegaire.

I answer the crowd's query. "Help is simple. Stop quarreling." They glance suspiciously at one another. I continue.

"Each of you are sons and daughter of

Eire, just as much as Deidre and the royal couple." Laegaire looks surprised. My words startle me as well, but I plunge forward.

"Each of you are sons and daughters of the Light, whether you call him Michael or Lugh."

Grumbles rise, but I press on as I climb the front pew bench and brandish my sword of Lugh. I feel the words surge through me.

"Our warriors of light engage Morgar, not to slay him, but to soften his heart, so he, too, like Morici, can use his talents for the good of all."

Sparks fly from my sword to the tip of Michael's blade.

"Help Fr. Malachy to nurture Deidre back to health. Go back to your homes and treat each other with respect. Forgive one another."

Martha comes to your side, Deidre. I see a tear in her eye. Eldonna holds her shoulders. I feel her warmth, a warmth I did not expect.

"Culain, I will take care of Deidre. Forgive me for me harshness with her. Truly she is a princess."

Caleb is obstinate. "She's no princess. This band is no different from the Abbess, Martha. They lie."

I can see the thick ice over his heart and shoulders. I place my sword gently on the thickest section. Steam billows. Caleb cries out -- not from any pain from the sword, but from the pain in his heart for his cruelty to you, sweet Deidre, the true princess. He sits on the wooden floor of the church and weeps openly. I put my hand on his shoulder.

"It's hard to face the hardness of our hearts and to see the mistakes we have made and the harm we have done, Caleb, but now is time for redemption."

The sobbing man reaches out to Martha. "I'm sorry for what I have done." He stands up and speaks to the crowd as he wipes away tears.

"Culain speaks the truth. She is the Princess. I pray that she recovers so that she can forgive me."

The other villagers cluster around Caleb. His repentance stuns them and they feel sympathy for him. I am surprised to see my "parents" there as well. I did not think they had this capacity for compassion. It touches me.

Colin McGee steps up.

"As messenger of the enchanted realm, I ask ye all to reflect on yer own hearts and reach out to our brave leaders and pray for them."

Fr. Malachy weaves his way to the center of the throng. "Friends, let us extend our hands in blessing to this holy crew." The assembly extends arms in our direction.

"May Deidre heal. May her adopted parents tend to her. May her compatriots carry on her cause." The energy rises. Light filters through the stained glass, illuminating the image of Michael. I hear pipe music in the distance.

I sense a voice urging me to move forward.

"Thank you, good people of St. Michael's, but we must leave you now." I place my sword upon your shoulder, Deidre, my friend.

"My princess of Ulster, we dedicate ourselves to bring freedom to your royal parents!" A cheer arises and this once ugly crowd smiles at us and claps our backs.

A new threat emerges as we exit the church.

Hawks circle overhead by the many dozens. I clench my teeth and grab my sword's hilt. They rush at us, striking like icy cannonballs. The first hawk knocks Colin to the ground before we can respond. When they see our flashing swords, they dive behind the church spires, knowing well that we will not strike above the church with you and the villagers inside.

Soft voices rise inside the church. The villagers are praying for us. Father Malachy has lit candles which each holds aloft. I feel their prayers without knowing the words. The candlelight and voices warm my heart and calm me. An idea flows into me. I put down my sword and pull out my flute and began to play faerie tunes and dance as I never had before. I feel Lugh's magic flow through my music.

Water begins to drip down the spires. The icy hawk exteriors melt rapidly. I help Colin up and he dances to my magical tune.

The abbesses also pull out their flutes. The sun shines more brightly, reminding me of the Enchanted Forest. The trickle of water becomes a torrent. The hawks, unencumbered, lose interest in harassing us or reporting to Morgar. They fly higher, as if dancing in the sky, until, at last, they disappear into the currents of the firmament.

I look inside the church doors. Caleb carries you with Martha at your side and with my adopted parents, Eldonna and Eamonn, behind them. I can see you breathing, and, for a moment, blink open your eyes, ever so briefly seeing me before lapsing back into a deep sleep. I feel hope that you will recover. I have underestimated the ability of our "parents" to support us.

"You do well, my friend." It is your voice dear, Deidre, that I hear in my mind. "May Lugh and Michael be with you." My heart rises.

I blow you a kiss and wave to the crew to alight the horses. I like the taste of a victory with music — without swords and sparks. My heart feels the warmth of loving hearts joined in music and dance. I treasure this experience.

The steeds whinny and take off like the wind toward Ards Forest. Overhead white-feathered Maeve and dark-feathered Morici and Ermanci give us a triple-winged escort. They guide us to our destiny with Morgar.

Chapter 8

The Journey

 s my heart aches, Deeder, it feels as though razor-sharp shards of ice dig into its soft red core. My father is lost just after I finally found him. Morgar and his hawks with sharp talons nearly destroyed you and Morici. The strength of Lugh is in my heart, but I also feel his pain, the pain of seeing those who you love suffer. As I ride my black mount that flies through the forest, I know the very Enchantment itself, home to Lugh, is in danger. He needs me. You and the royal family need me. Eire needs me to defend her. But I am just 10 years old. I feel my heart sag under the weight. The pain burns my lungs.

Laegaire's steed roars up next to me. I

feel his horse's breath on my leg and its sweat as its bruising thigh brushes my foot in passing. I turn and stared into the master's eyes. "Culain, your heart can melt the icy fears that cut its flesh. Trust your heart's pulse. Feel it." His eyes glow with fire, an inextinguishable energy, like small suns. His fiery look resonates like cathedral bells ringing. The icy needles in my heart melt into a sea of refreshing water that that begins to wash over the pain.

"Culain, know that Lugh is with you." He pulls out his sword. It flashes and sparkles in the night like Chinese fireworks as he bolts ahead. I breathe in the crisp rushing air as it fills my lungs and expands my chest. As jets of steam exhaust from the horses' nostrils, as it does mine. I sit upright in my saddle. A misty breath funnels out of my mouth as I dig my heels into the warm flanks of horseflesh. As I gain and pass Laegaire, images of the Enchanted Forest dance in my brain.

I visualize my lonely quest in the Ards Forest when I was separated from you, Deidre. I recall the sword standing in the path next to the bank of the river Veritas. That vibrant sword flowed so easily into my grasp.

Mists rose and encircled Emerald Mountain. I saw what I had not yet revealed to you, my friend. There was no Morici in my lonely quest. My foe was Morgar! He too was encased in ice but, unlike Morici, he was free to move about, big as a lion and quick as a gazelle. He despised me for the power of the sword of Lugh. Yet no matter how fast he moved, I was a step ahead of him. No matter where he struck with lightning, the sword of Lugh deflected it. And when he did strike home, Lugh the sword merely absorbed its lightning and grew brighter. I thought Morgar would be afraid, but he was a worthy foe, adeptly avoiding my strikes. But gradually, icy shard by icy shard,

I disarmed him of some of the hatred and greed he had built up over many years. He slipped into Veritas, howling out violent threats as the current carried him away and out of the Enchantment. He vowed out loud that he would return. And, sadly, now he has.

I feel a new shard in my heart. I hear the voices of the faeries and leprechauns. They call out for my protection. Tears fill my eyes. This time I must complete the battle. For too long have the powers of darkness ruled in Eire and contaminated the forest, even the Enchanted One. Someone must stand up to the scourge. Deidre, my friend, it is you who give me the courage to engage again as you did with Morici. And, yes, Deidre, I listen to Gabrielle, who speaks from my heart just as she does for you. And I hear Lugh's music sing from my sword. There is no turning back.

(I am sorry, dear Deidre, that only now are you hearing these thoughts that I share, but Lugh bade me so. He knows that each of us must first battle the darkness alone in our own way to overcome it. It is our free will to choose to open the door to light or to be imprisoned by darkness. I knew that my duty was not yet done. Deidre, you drew upon your love to melt the chasm between you and Morici. Now it is my turn to melt the chasm between Morgar and me.)

Maeve flies overhead with Ermanci, one above each of Laegaire's shoulders, like an honor guard. Morici rides up next to me, unknowing still of my battle with her father. The pounding hooves ricochet thunderous claps into the woods. I smell the musty peat and rich earth. The land is coming alive in our presence, emanating musky aromas, breathing out life-filling breezes, enveloping us in a canopy of oaken roots, trunks, and leaf-strewn branches. The very voice of Eire echoes and spurs us onward.

(I know what none of the crew behind me knows, but what, you, Deidre, surely guessed in your heart. In my battle with Morgar, I came face to face with myself as time stopped. I entered Morgar's heart and sensed with mine that even in his deepest pain, this dark Ice King, like Morici, possesses a hidden spark of love that surpasses and mutes all the pain and darkness.)

I know that no matter how great the evil Morgar wields against us, it ultimately is no match for the spark of Light, the spark of Lugh, the fire of Love. Even knowing this, however, past suffering pierces me with heartache. My mount slows and the other riders begin to pass me again as pungent tufts of peat and earth pelt my face with earthy blackness. Its coolness opens me to Lugh and his words.

"My dear Culain, all of your ancestors lived, suffered and died in Ireland in the anticipation of your coming. My son, you and Deidre have come to know your deepest heart and to trust it. Yes, there has been much pain and death. Yes, Culain, there will be more. But each one who dies offers up his or her life that those who carry the Light, like you, may touch the hearts of those who live now, but remain in the deepest sleep."

Lugh flies overhead, behind the others. But how can he fly? The others do not see or hear him. Lugh has no wings, but wings thrash the air with a broad wingspan. The second face appears. Lugh's twin, Michael, the Archangel, holds him with one arm and brandishes his sword with the other. They drop back next to me so I see and feel the presence and warm glow of giants.

"We will protect and defend you, Culain, against all the snares of darkness, even the very fears that pierce icy nails into your heart." Fire lights their eyes with a glow brighter than Laegaire's. My heart rises and tears well in my eyes. I grab my sword and hold it overhead. It discharges a brilliant purple light that splits into two beams and meets with the swords of Lugh and Michael. I feel full and whole again. My protectors disappear as I hear the faint tune of Lugh.

I dig my heels into my steed, and storm ahead of the pack. The wind and I are one. I feel like an eagle soaring. I feel like Light.

The calls rail behind me to wait for them, but I know that it is my destiny, my charge to be the first to engage. Deidre, your heart knows how this can feel. Your presence is at my side. I surge ahead until their voices fade behind me. I am the Wind.

A bolt of lightning strikes me to the

ground!

No warning clouds, no hawks, no sign or sense of Morgar. But, as I sit sprawled upon the ground, I am unharmed, but my back aches any my head spins. I sensed the fear in my horse as I fell and now I watch it gallop away as I sit up.

The blackest of crows lands on my shoulder. Its talons squeeze me gently and its charcoal wings brush my cheek, knocking off muddy earth. The cackles melt into Morici's voice.

"Young Culain, we are allies, but you must not make the same mistake as I did. It is not just your battle with the dark forces of Morgar. It's all of ours. We must stay together, or he will elude us again just as he did me when I fell into vengefulness."

The words strike me with an enchanting wisdom that penetrates the wounds of my heart. I pat this crow, this Enchanter, as I whistle to my frightened mount. He knows my call and begins to prance eagerly back to me.

"You speak truth, Morici. Now is the time

that we must re-connect with one another." The others catch up, even Morici's rider-less mount.

"Morici is right, my good friends, we must stay together for the sake of the Enchanted Kingdom."

"And for yers, Culain!" Maeve's voice is stern.

"Culain, Morici didn't strike you from your horse. I did! Morgar is waiting for us at Ankara's gate. Ankara has suffered enough. And you will be vulnerable to Morgar's power there. There's another way in, but we must go through the banshee forest. Follow me, all of you!" The word "banshee" echoes in the air. A shiver of concern arises.

The abbesses look skeptically at one another and pull their horses back. Colin is just behind Brigit and flashes a fearful look. Laegaire looks ready. Ermanci lands on my other shoulder. Maeve flies above us, wings extended like an eagle's.

"Fear not, me friends, the banshees may wail and keen but they know us as friends.

They too are faeries!" She flies in front of us into a cave hidden behind some gorse. I dismount and follow her. The rest of the Resistance follows me.

Even as I walk down the dark damp halls of the cave I see a luminescence in the walls that is unlike normal Ulster caves. Moisture drips from the ceiling and splatters like lonesome teardrops into dark pools on the cave's earthen floor. A brackish odor of mold and decay causes us to cover our noses. I preferred the other entrance, even with its deep cavernous fall. Then we hear them. The ear-piercing banshee keens and wails echo in the distance. We cover our ears, but the cries are fierce. The pungent odor then fills our nostrils and brings goose bumps to our arms. Much to our chagrin, Maeve waves us forward. I am glad to be just a follower. The light from the walls and the floors has a greenish hue. Many spots now have little pads of moss even though I can see no openings for sunlight. As the waves of sound subside, the brightness in the distance dances between Maeve's wings.

As we emerge in a lush meadow, the

deepness of green and the brightness of the sun force us to rub our eyes and behold the bedazzling splendor of the Enchantment. The fresh crisp air sweetly fills our lungs. Several oaks nearby speak immediately.

"Maeve, ye and yer band must move quickly! We expect the keening to begin again any moment." As though prophetic, a banshee appears before us with a hideous scowl and tattered veil, drenched in tears. She flies like a bat in my direction. I reach for my sword, but the keening stops as she sees me.

"Culain, I am Isis, the banshee of Deidre's clan, the Conalls."

"Is Deidre alright, Isis?"

"Yes, Culain, but ye must rid the Enchantment of Morgar. The very fabric of our kingdom is threatened." The ground begins to tremble beneath out feet.

"Morgar holds the Enchanted Castle hostage." Colin McGee surges forward.

"We must save them!" Maeve grabs his shoulder to hold him back.

"Remember, it will take all of us to deal

with Morgar. We must stick together."

"She's right!" It is not Isis who speaks, but a banshee who looks more worn and more drenched with tears. Isis puts a hand upon her shoulder.

"Culain, this is Morgana, the banshee of yer clan."

I am speechless. Like you, Deidre, I do not know the name of my clan. I only know my father as Sultain.

Maeve turns to me, but speaks to the banshee.

"It is time, Morgana."

"Ye are of the clan of Patrick."

"The Patrick of the church?" Bewildered, I step back.

"The very same! The clan that had roots in Britannia, but chose Eire as a new home to love and defend."

"But didn't Patrick speak out against the Old Religion?"

"Only when it was used for dark purposes. He spoke out against all dark purposes. His only goal was to love and defend Eire. And he loved all the enchanting creatures in it."

Now I understand why it is both Lugh and Michael that lead me to this place with their protection. Indeed, it is the light of <u>both</u> the Old and the New Religions that guides me. It is the same light. My discoveries are interrupted by Morgana's wail.

"Ye must proceed, my dear Culain. The power of darkness rises in this very Enchantment. If ye do not go soon, ye too will suffer Sultain's fate."

Isis steps forward. "Go, now, my friends. The very life of Enchantment depends on yer actions. Take courage from the ancestors of Patrick and Conall."

I hug Morgana and Isis and charge forward. Maeve holds me back by my shoulder. Laegaire steps forward ahead of me.

"Heed their guidance, but let me lead." Laegaire's billowing cloak lifts in the breeze and his shadowy form shows more clarity and texture. I yield to his wisdom. The abbesses follow us. Morici and Ermanci fly overhead on either side of Maeve. The banshee forest is quiet, except for our footsteps. As I look ahead, I see Emerald Mountain covered by a white mist. Dark clouds form in the distance in the direction of the Faerie Sand Castle.

Lightning illuminates the sky. Rolling thunder shakes the leaves of the oaks. Peace rises in my heart as I am surrounded by these strong, loving members of the Resistance. Surely, we will prevail.

Just as we emerge from the clearing and hear the gentle ripples of Veritas flowing beside us, I see a friend I met before, a friend you know, Deidre. The tall and proud Osiris. The broad Oak's branches rise to greet us and he spreads a wide, barky smile.

The warmth of the Oaks fills me and I run to his trunk and embrace him like the old friend he is.

"So, the brave wee lad returns to visit Osiris. The last time ye hardly noticed me."

I feel a twinge of guilt as I recall almost ignoring this sentinel of the Enchanted Forest.

His bark is firm and warm. His wide branches sweep in around me like the skirts of the abbesses. The others laugh as I dance about Osiris' trunk.

"So yer band here is going to kick out that imposter of an enchanter, Morgar, eh, Culain?"

"That's our goal, Osiris." He brushes me back.

"That's OOOOsiris, lad. Some respect, boy!" I laugh despite myself at this sensitive old oak.

"I have something for ye, lad. And for Deidre, too." I cannot imagine what it is.

"It's over there in the ground. There are two of them."

Indeed, there are two oak seedlings with small green leaves. These tiny sentinels-to-be were the only oaks nearby.

"These oaks are blessed by Ankara and myself. They'll be able to grow outside the Enchantment. They'll grow in yer darker world and will bring life and light to it."

Such glee springs from the oak's voice

that I can nearly touch its warmth. Despite the urgency of our mission, the others gather round. Colin produces a little shovel. Each of the abbesses have an empty pouch that I can fill with a seedling and some earth.

"Now promise me, lad, will ye care for these wee oaks, for they're the promise of Eire? They'll be there to support ye and Deidre and re-build the kingdom blessed by Tara."

With tears in my eyes, I promise in the name of Lugh, Michael, and Patrick.

And, Deidre, I promise on your behalf. Then I gently dig the young oaks and nestle one in each of the two pouches.

I give Osiris a hug.

"Here, here!" come the shouts around me along with laughter and clapping. Maeve then steps forward.

"Thank ye, kind sentinel Osiris, but storms brew in the distance. Culain, bid yer friend adieu, for we must go now." I dance a quick jig as I pipe a short song around the tree and then lead the band, piping all the way, in the direction of Emerald Mountain. Osiris waves his branches with such a flourish that several leaves float down upon us and are swirled into the rising wind.

As we wave back, a billowy thunderhead climbs in the distant sky, growing darker with each step. Our music stops and we pick up our pace as the drops of rain begin to pound and the rolls of thunder boom in the distance. The abbess's skirts now look more like sails and I grab each of their hands to help them press against the onslaught of the wind. My arms strain to resist the force. The rising storm brings goose bumps that tingle my skin.

The next thing I know a blinding bolt of lightning strikes only feet away from us. The sweet smell of watermelon fills my nostrils from the struck air. The lightning's ferocity makes my hands shake and my feet freeze to the ground. The dizzying feeling fades when another bolt strikes behind us.

An eerie crack of timber gives little doubt of where the strike hit. A shrill cry rises from Osiris and his trunk splits in two, blackened and burning.

The abbesses try to hold me back, but I run faster than the lightning to him.

He whispers to me as he expires and my tears mingle with the rain.

"Even the darkest powers of Morgar can never destroy the Enchantment, if only ye hold it safely in yer heart. Tell Deidre to remember me. I will rise again."

Then there is only the smell of burnt wood and the black of ashes turning to a sea of mud upon the earth.

I do not know if I can bear it.

Yes, Deidre, we indeed must both remember the wondrous Osiris.

Chapter 9

Destiny

he acrid charred remains of Osiris melt my heart, Deidre. You must know the feeling from the lightning strike that ripped Ankara apart. My heart tells me to trust, even though the stench turns my stomach. Too many have fallen to the bitter hate of the Donns and their Milesian ancestors. My Tuatha core tells me that my sword will guide me. I yearn to charge Emerald Mountain.

"Breathe, Culain, deeply and slowly." Maeve wraps her wings around me as I follow her instruction. With each breath, new tears form and her wings give me a security, an isolation, in which I feel safe in crying, tear after tear. The sweaty flow gives a bitter, salty pungency to my mouth. Then the mucus comes, a flowing river of sorrow--- not just for Osiris, but also for my father, for you Deidre, for the faeries and leprechauns now imprisoned, and for the King and Queen. I feel powerless, but gain power. I feel isolated, but connected to my lineage, to Lugh, to the light. I feel weak, but grow in strength. I feel a purging, a cleansing of sorrow and fear. My chest heaves. My lip quivers. My body feels heavy, but lightens with each tear and each emanation from my mouth and my nose. I am a sight, dear Deidre, but no one sees me. Even Maeve just holds me with her eyes closed. I feel her warmth touching my heart. It is like an electrical charge. I feel it flow through my body and ground me to the earth. I grab the sleeve of my tunic and wipe away the tears and blow my nose into the kerchief Colin gave me. I remember that I am not alone, that all the burden of challenging Morgar is not only m quest this time. I call upon your presence, Deidre, and I feel your heart as well.

Raindrops begin to pelt the charred wood of Osiris' trunk with a cleansing effect. A new sooty, but fragrant, smell rises from the broken black trunk and emerges as a sizzling smoky mist. The smell is sweet not acrid. No longer is it like burning peat or wood. The aromatic ashes of the Holy Oak calm me. I feel Osiris' presence in my lungs as I breathe it in. As Maeve unwraps her wings I have full view of the fallen sentry. Jagged shards, burst bark, and even some of the unscarred core rings of this ancient leader. My friends gather round me, pelted by the near waterfall of rain now pouring from the raven-black sky. Thunder and flash roll in the distance, but are ebbing. Morici strokes the remaining trunk that still stands. Her caress is warm and tender, like the heart that has opened in her. Laegaire sits on the largest fallen branch, almost hidden among the leaves, as his head tilts forward, bowed in a silent prayer. The abbesses kneel in the mud and hold each other, wrapped in love and sadness. Ermanci flies from branch to branch, calling out as if to tell Osiris to rise again.

I grab some of the charred wood and smear it across my forehead, my face and my arms as the wind dies down and the rain now is a light drizzle. Then I take the black chalk and draw a six-pointed star on the foreheads of each warrior and, finally, Maeve herself.

"This is the sign of Osiris, the sign of the

star of David. It also is the sign of Lugh, the sign of starlight. Let it guide us in saving the Enchantment."

My words are complete. Laegaire rises, staff in one hand, sword in the other. One by one they arise, each with a sword of light bristling in front of them like sparkling fire, only the colors are brilliant violets, vibrant pinks, and fiery orange. The illuminations dance above us and around us like the plume of a peacock.

Maeve speaks, "Me friends, we did not reach Emerald Mountain as planned, trying to draw Morgar away from the Castle. This vile attack by Morgar here on the sacred ground of Osiris' roots tells us he will stop at nothing. Our only hope is to combine our powers and head directly to the Enchanted Castle. Whatever we do, we must protect the good faeries and leprechauns under Morgar's dark spell. The survival of the Enchantment is at stake. Our friends are in mortal danger. Let us press forward and draw upon the Light."

Maeve leads the way. Laegaire and Morici flank her. Their eyes are almost as bright as their swords. They call upon the enchanting power of Lugh's tune, singing aloud and waving us to join them:

"O beloved Eire we come to thee,

One for all, all for one, all in unity.

Our hearts yearn for the Enchantment.

Only deliverance will make us content.

We know the true ancient power--

The Love in which we flower."

The abbesses and I join in and hold our

swords higher. Their energy lifts me. I feel alive and vibrant to be with such friends even as we trudge in the mud and muck and soot.

The energy from the lifted swords spreads out a glowing, encapsulating plume that repels the droplets of water. I feel the light weave in and out like an intricate and delicate silk fabric. It sustains our singing voices. It fills our rising hearts. It dries our grieving tears. We are one. And the aroma that fills my lungs tastes of sweet bursts of holy oak. My spattered feet feel as if I walk on air. It is not long before the great turrets of the Enchanted Castle appear in the distance. The dark pall of gloom in the sky hangs over the sandy towers like the muck of peat after working in the bogs. Black as a moonless night. Thick as molasses. Cold and damp like breath-stifling consumption.

Then I see the dark enchanter's cape billowing as his solitary figure stands with a tall staff at the peak of the highest tower. He sucks in the darkness around him. Or is he spewing it forth? I cannot see the face, but I know the hardened heart and the icy visage. It can only be Morgar!

The attack of hawks is swift. They swarm in the thousands. Never have I seen such an assembly of screeching warrior birds. They looked almost like eagles in size, yet they fly with the speed of ghosts.

The sky simply becomes hawk. The swarm amasses around our band and begins diving at us. At first, the glow of our energy bubble repels them. They fall back as though they have hit armor. We charge forward with a greater pace, but there are too many.

"Help!" Abbess Margaret has fallen to the ground and several hawks are ripping their talons into her skirts and tearing at her hair. I rush to her side, sword extended. The sword almost carries me as if I too am a bird. Then emerald sparks charge from the sword and pulse with direct hits to every hawk that surrounds Margaret. Still I can see the blood oozing from her forehead. She faints into a pool of blood. I instinctively grab my whitest, purest faerie dust and sprinkle it over her as the hawks keep attacking and my sword keeps repelling.

As I look around I see Laegaire's cap

flying in the air. The hawks are ripping and tearing it. Then Laegaire lifts his sword in the direction of his hat. The hat doubles in size and begins to fly like a live eagle, buffeting hawks in every direction. Ermanci, too, looks like he had grown into a bird of prey as he chases away hawks with a vengeance.

Then I feel the sharp piercing at my neck. Two hawks are nearly lifting me off the ground. A third rips shreds in the back of my tunic and I feel the hot flush of my blood trickle down my back. I cry out in deep, mournful pain. I feel barely conscious as the talons dig deeper into my neck. My sword falls to the ground. I see new attackers heading toward Margaret but there is nothing I can do. Darkness fills my eyes and I feel a buzzing in my ears and a flush upon my face.

As I begin to fade from consciousness, falling toward Margaret, I feel a sudden grip upon my arms and the warm folds of the Abbess Brigit's cloak. Her strong arms lift me as if I am a feather. I faintly hear the squeal of hawks and feel the release of talons. But the gushing of blood is too much. I pass out.

A rude slap on my cheek awakens me. I open my hazy eyes to see the face of Morici.

"Culain, this is not your time to fall. Rise up." She chants ancient words and signs my forehead with the six-pointed star. She rubs emerald salve on my neck and back. I begin to breathe with broken coughs and the searing pain from the talon's wounds. But I struggle to my feet and pick up my sword. I see new gaping openings in the shield of hawks and the gaps are widening.

I have never seen Queen Maeve in all her beauty and power. Her image is stunning. I put my hand over my eyes to dim the brightness. Like a brilliant angel, she is full of light and the size of a dozen eagles with a wingspan as wide as Osiris was tall. She cuts a swath through the throng of dark hawks as though they are pebbles in her way. Dark feathers and dark bodies fall from the sky. She extends her sword and its light shines-- a mini-sun, sparking orbs of pink, orange and purple that further press away the dark throng.

"Culain, come this way!" It is Brigit. Her strong arms support me as we tread around the stunned hawks. I see the others, moving swiftly toward the castle, even the Abbess Margaret, supported by Morici. The healing power of a great enchantress is magical. I am so glad, Deidre, that you helped Morici to know her love and join us. My breath is short but I follow my wondrous companions toward the darkening castle.

As I stumble across a hawk, nearly falling, the earth trembles. Brigit holds me upright. Thunderous booms come from the castle. I see one of the turret peaks totter. It falls, crashing like a small avalanche over the side of the tower. We still are too distant to see much. The mist is thick and the sky almost as dark as night. My heart falls as I see the destroyer. The solitary figure in a black cloak stands like a rigid sentinel at the top staircase of the castle entrance. Lightning flashes extend from his staff and his eyes, but he remains unmoved, spraying sparks around like the hands of a steeple clock, grinding around rigidly with cold metal gears.

Suddenly he moves – swiftly -- behind the gates, clanging them shut behind him.

"Be gone, dark intruder, from me castle!" Queen Maeve's voice booms over the meadow and all about. Light glows from her form that is bright enough to cast shadows. And her bolts blast the spot where Morgar had been into an explosion of sand, earth, and stone. I can no longer see Morgar, but Maeve advances quickly.

The sky lights up with such a torrent of

lightning flashes that, at first, I think it is the sun. I think these flashes are from Maeve, but I am wrong! Maeve's wings are struck and she begins to fall, but somehow, regains flight just before crashing into her own iron gate. Her sword extends now and she deflects the powerful charges directly into the gate and pulverizes it into molten metal and sand. Morgar's cloak ripples in the winds and he runs into the large oak doors of the main castle gate.

A small bird flies just behind Maeve. Laegaire calls out to them both.

"Maeve, Ermanci, wait for us to re-inforce you! We must work together against his dark power."

The voice seems to carry on the winds even though we are many furlongs from the castle. I can almost see the words aloft in the air, carrying themselves to the flying creatures.

Ermanci bumps into the diving Maeve and starts to crash to the ground. Maeve swoops down and snatches him up and lands on the steps just below the oak doors. The rest of us strain to reach them. Laegaire is nearly there. I am regaining strength, not far behind.

Morici shape-shifts into a crow and reaches Maeve and Ermanci's side.

"We're coming!" Brigit holds a tired Margaret up as they press resolutely forward.

A bolt strikes just in front of the abbesses. Then I find out who I really am. A voice from my heart speaks softly. "The sword!"

I extend it and chant repeatedly: "Lugh, Lugh, Lugh!"

I meet each bolt from the sky with a deflecting bolt from my sword. No thinking. I am not sure what it is happening. I just let the sword do its appointed work.

Morgar is getting frustrated. He pushes out a whole band of leprechauns, held in check by his hawks as he snarls a threat.

"This castle is mine, ye fools. Any more of yer tricks and these wee people will never know the Enchantment again."

As Morgar faces Maeve, Morici, and Ermanci – circling about him, I slip into a side passage Colin has shown me. I let the sword lead me through the hall and behind Morgar.

I see him raise his staff menacingly at the flyers in front of him. Again, I do not think. I just follow the sword.

Never have I seen a sword of Lugh do anything like this. A purplish-blue charge spreads like a wave from the tip of the sword like a net of energy. It flies like a bird and drapes itself over Morgar.

He spins at me and charges.

"No child can defeat me!" he fumes, but his steps grow heavy.

The net wraps around him like a serpent. He starts having trouble breathing. His staff shatters into matchsticks. He falls to the ground, gasping.

The words just come to me. I do not think them.

"You will surrender to the power of Lugh, the power of the Enchantment."

I hear flute music ring in my ears. It is Lugh's tune, Deidre, but I sense you in the music. Tears are forming in Morgar's eyes as he begins to writhe on the ground as the purplish net tightens around him. He is powerless.

He can only whisper. "I yield to Lugh!"

The purple cloak dissolves. The clouds part for rays of sun that drench us with a white glow. Maeve, Laegaire, Morici, and Ermanci grab the weak and powerless Morgar and lead him away.

The faeries come from all corners and the leprechauns throng around me.

"Long live Culain, the Hero of Lugh, the Hero of Eire!"

They begin to carry me in the air, but I do not smile.

I sense that the Darkness has only receded.

Deidre, I hear your cry, so the story flies back to you. Continue...

Chapter 10

Dark Dreams

Deidre continues to Culain...

 ulain, I am sure Fr. Malachy's intentions are pure, but the church factions are beyond his control. As the heat of fever fills me with sweats and chills, I wonder if all is real or nightmare until I hear the clackety-clack of those dreaded shoes. Each step makes my head throb to the core. By some miracle, the good priest manages to persuade her to remove her shoes as she paces to and fro around me. I know this woman I called "Mum" truly cares about me in the depths of her heart. Her icy hardness separates her from her own deeper caring and compassion. Martha and Caleb bicker about whether to bring a compress for my head. Culain, as my head throbs, I send my prayer to you for help. I do expect that you hear it. Then I lose consciousness for a wee bit, drifting into a fuzzy haze.

Awakening from sometimes tortuous dreams, I feel the wet drench of my own sweat-- like I had just been thrown into a river. I push away the blankets that Caleb keeps trying to put back on me. The harsh heat of the fever oppresses me. I long to cool down.

"I have an apothecary for ye, dear Deidre. Sit up now."

I recognize the voice as your mother, Culain. Eldonna is gentler than I remember. She looks sober. Her hair is brushed. She even wears a clean tunic. She has some herbs on a wooden spoon mixed with liquid. I look in her eyes and see only genuine concern. I swallow the awful potion. It makes me cough. She gives me sips of water. I ask her to sponge my face with water. And my hands, arms and feet as well. I feel on fire. I cough again.

Then I see your Da, Culain. Eamonn too looks sober. He helps me sit up and puts his ear to my chest and asks me to take a deep breath. He moves his ear to different spots and has me breath again. It makes me feel faint. I ask him to stop.

"Okay, Deidre. Lay back." He too picks up a wet cloth. They remove all the blankets and began sponging my skin to cool the fever.

Fr. Malachy hovers with Martha and Caleb.

"What is it, Eamonn? What ails her?" I hear genuine concern.

"She's got congestion of the lungs. I have seen it before. The herbs Eldonna gave her will help break the fever and assist her body in fighting whatever is invading her lungs."

I do not let on that I hear every word. I remember farmer Murphy dying of this illness a few months ago. He was a strapping man of 35 years and it felled him like a tree to an axe. For a moment, the memory shakes me. I shiver not from the illness, but from fear.

Weakly I whisper, "Eamonn."

He brings his ear close to my face.

"There's a white powder in my pouch. It's enchanted."

He pulls back just for a moment, then takes a deep breath and comes closer.

"Sprinkle some over my chest and say: in the name of Danu begin to heal."

He struggles at first to find the proper white powder. He looks at me and hesitates.

"Trust me, Eamonn." My voice is weak, but clear.

As he reaches his hand over my chest, Caleb wrenches it back with a bellow.

"What kind of evil magic are ye tryin', Eamonn. No dark spells for me Deidre!"

I reach out my hand to Caleb's leg. He kneels and comes close.

"It's all right, Da. Let him do it." I see, for the first time ever, a small tear for me in the corner of his eye. I know he struggles to accept that faerie dust is not evil. But, I see, for the first time, a willingness to open his mind — and his heart.

"Let it be then, Eamonn. Do as she says." I am proud of him and can feel the hardness of his heart softening as he holds my hand and speaks.

"We'll make it up to ye, wee one. Please get better now." He blows his nose with an old tattered kerchief and makes room for Eamonn.

As the powder falls and the words weave their magic, I feel a calming coolness begin to cleanse the feverish temperatures and to allow my lungs to open. The results are not instant, but finally I can sleep – deeply. No longer do I hear voices or feel the touch of sponging cloths. I drift off into a quiet world of peaceful nothingness. A gratefulness fills me for the gentle care from those whom I have forsaken of such kindness. This feeling permeates my slumber.

Then I drift into strange, dark dreams…

I run through the Enchanted Forest calling out to you, Culain. I need to warn you. Of what, I am not sure. I call out. It feels real, like I am with you in the Enchantment, not lying asleep in St. Michael's. Lugh appears in front of me, flute in hand, towering over the trees. He plays his lilting music, winks at me, encouraging me to follow his example. At first, I resist and call out to Lugh, imploring him.

"Lugh, we must help Culain. I know he's in danger. We all love him dearly. Please help him."

Then hawks begin to fly at me with talons extended, but I am not afraid. I follow Lugh's lead and pull out my pipe and we begin to play our songs together. The dark birds scratch at my hair. They rip holes in my tunic. Still I play on and move forward, deeper into the forest, toward The Enchanted Castle. Lugh is no longer visible, but his music resonates with mine. As we get closer, I hear cries in the distance, cries of the faeries, cries of the leprechauns. I can barely stand it. I continue to play, louder and louder. The hawks keep attacking me, even pulling me to the ground, but the music protects me. No blood flows. I get up and keep going forward. The music strengthens me.

My thoughts sing out to you, my dear friend Culain. I call upon all the powers of the Enchantment, all the love of Eire, all the strength of our Ancestors, to give you the protection you will need to be our Champion, to be the Defender of Eire that you are – with all our support, with all our love. My desires meld with the music and I press forward.

Nacham flies in front of me and catches my attention. His feathers are tattered. His flight is drunken. Tears cover his face.

"Help me, Deidre." I pull the flute from my mouth and reach out to him. I swat the hawks with my flute. I pull Nacham close to me and thrash yet another hawk with my flute before bringing it again to my mouth to join Lugh's music.

Gabrielle bursts into view. Never have I seen her look so large or so strong. She is so full of light that she looks like a white eagle, sleek and strong. When the hawks see her, they try to attack, but the sheer force of her light repels them with an invisible shield. She flies higher, drawing the chase of the hawks and leaves us safe to move forward.

As I look up, her voice rings out forcefully. "In the name of Lugh and in the name of Danu, I banish you from this place!" Her words are clear and firm.

Waves of light appear to emanate from her. Each wave strikes the hawks with the force of a strong wind, knocking them back, creating confusion. Soon they are crashing into each other. They begin to panic and flee. Suddenly the scene is quiet.

Pained cries echo in the distance and tears well in my eyes. Gabrielle flies in front of Nacham and me. We press forward to the castle. Song fills the air — mine and Lugh's, but the cries of our enchanted friends reveal the dark danger that is consuming the Enchanted Forest. Never had I thought this possible. We press on, Culain, as I call out to you.

Then I awake in the church. The tumult has stopped. Martha is wiping my forehead as the sweat of fever trickles from my brow.

Fr. Malachy is holding my hand. As though the dream still possesses me, I cry out!

"Culain! Watch out for the hawks!" The poor priest looks a bit shaken.

"He's not here, me dear girl. There are no hawks, sweet Deidre. Ye're safe. We've been praying for both of ye."

I sit up and look at those around me. Where are

they — Lugh, the hawks, Nacham, Gabrielle, the cries of the faeries? Culain, I fear for you and the Enchanted Castle.

I shiver and speak firmly to Fr. Malachy and Martha.

"None of us are safe if Morgar defeats Culain!"

Chapter 11

Unity

 am grateful that my fever breaks, but the strength of my dreams drains me. Eamonn and Eldonna give me water and more herbs. Their attentions calm me, but still Culain's safety captures my thoughts. The images of attacking hawks and the cries of the faeries haunt me. Is Morgar's power too great for Culain?

Fr. Malachy holds my hands and views my eyes with a gentle gaze. His face glows unusually bright. The rays of the sun reflect the colors of St. Michael's stained-glass image onto Fr. Malachy's face. I sense that the strength of St. Michael in battle is that same strength that is with Culain.

"Deidre, I've seen a sign from St. Michael himself. Look."

I see a dove flying about inside the church, above St. Michael's statue. It rests upon the edge of his outstretched sword. The dove holds a shamrock in its beak. Flying to Fr. Malachy, the bird drops the three-leafed shamrock on his shoulder and flies away, almost as if it is disappearing into air as I cannot follow its departure. Fr. Malachy takes the shamrock and gives it to me.

"Culain is safe. Surely this is a sign of peace." The good priest crosses himself solemnly and kisses me on the forehead. His trust in St. Michael is beginning to rub off on me.

Caleb and Martha help me sit up, propping me up with some sacks of grain that were donated to the church. They each hug me. Eamonn and Eldonna give me hugs as well. We all feel hope, but part of me still seeks more signs that Culain is safe. The logic of Nacham in me wants proof, more tangible proof, that Fr. Malachy is right.

I hear a whisper in my ear. "Do not let the fever make you forget, my dear Deidre. Trust your heart."

Gabrielle's voice reassures me, but I am still impatient. I struggle to get up on my feet, but nearly fall. Fr. Malachy catches me.

"Take me to the door, Father, I need to look outside."

He knows that he cannot dissuade me. He and Caleb each take one of my arms.

As the door opens, I look up to the sky for signs. I see some starlings and wrens, but no predators fly through the treetops. I ask them to walk me down the steps into the brightness of the sun. My legs feel like noodles.

Then the darkness of my dreams boldly arrives in the now. A hawk screeches and barrels into me, nearly knocking me to the ground, even though both men hold me tightly. Then another strikes Caleb's ear, drawing fresh crimson blood. A third predator rips the rosary beads that Fr. Malachy carries around his neck. Dozens attack relentlessly until I am on the ground alone. The men are batting away the birds, protecting me. These are no signs of peace.

Then a strong breeze rises, pushing the tree branches down and altering the flight of the hawks. It grows stronger. Many of the hawks turn away. I hear the rush of great wings, wings that spread as wide as trees. It is Queen Maeve in all her majesty! The force of air from her wings and her very presence panic the remainder of the hawks. I can tell from her ruffled feathers, however, that she has recently been engaged in battle. The hawks sense it as well and want no part of her as they all hustle away.

Caleb's and Fr. Malachy's jaws nearly drop to the ground.

"But this cannot be!" They rub their eyes.

"I am Maeve, Queen of the Enchantment. My good pastor and Caleb, thank ye for protecting Deidre, but now is the time for her to come back with me to the Enchanted Castle. Culain has helped us to defeat Morgar."

Shouts of joy came from Eamonn, Eldonna, Martha and the others who had come from inside the church. Even though they too are in awe of Maeve, her news cheers them nonetheless.

"Be calm, me friends, for this is only one battle won, even though it is an important victory. Brugh Donn still rules. The Darkness still reigns as ye can see." Maeve's words strike home to Caleb who covers his bleeding ear and Fr. Malachy who gathers his broken rosary.

"Me friends, continue to help one another and to forgive one another. Let go of any hardness in yer hearts, for that is what gives power to the Darkness. It is only the love in yer hearts that can melt it. Deidre has shown us the way to trust in the loving power of the Enchantment. Follow her example."

They gather in a circle around me, hugging me and one another. The words of Queen Maeve finally dispel my worries about the battle, but I wonder if indeed I deserve her praise. I still feel weak. I still wonder if I am strong enough to help.

Fr. Malachy speaks for the group. "May God's grace go with ye, Deidre."

I see Maeve's wings flutter. I move slowly to her with the good pastor's help. He even wraps the retied rosary around my neck. I climb into her embrace and she lifts me into the air with grace and speed. I wave weakly to those below. Being with Maeve fills me with a renewed vigor and strength.

"Is everyone alright, Maeve?"

"A few talon wounds, but everyone is safe, Deidre, thanks in part to yer presence."

"My presence?"

"We heard ye piping the song of Lugh. We heard ye calling Lugh to us."

"But that was just in my dream."

"In the Enchantment, me dear, there is little difference between dream and reality."

"So, I really helped in the battle?"

"Yes, Deidre, it was yer love for Culain and the others that sustained us when Morgar's power was at its peak."

I cry tears of happiness and relief. I yearn to see and embrace my friends.

Two dark birds appear ahead of us. At first, I pull back, fearing another hawk, but then I recognize the birds.

Morici calls out to us.

"Deidre, we come to escort you to the castle."

She and Ermanci take positions on either side of me.

Maeve looks at me with concern.

"Dear Deidre, we are going to take a different route across the veil between Eire and the Enchantment. I will tell ye more of the Oval Gate later. But ye are weak now and I am casting a spell of dreamless sleep over ye, so that ye can rest and regain some strength. Close yer eyes." Then she sings an old Irish lullaby:

> *"Well I love thee,*
>
> *Smooth thou, soft thou!*
>
> *I too companion thee,*
>
> *I too lull thee.*
>
> *Soft thou! Soft thou!*
>
> *Soft my little love!*
>
> *Soft as silk to thee*
>
> *The heart of thy mother!"*

I drift off as more verses float by my ears and settle into the comfort of her strong arms. I know that Maeve is not my mother, but it feels as though she is. The magic of her voice takes me to a place of quiet that does not know the crossing of the veil between worlds. I feel refreshed when I finally awake as we enter the Enchantment. The dark clouds of my dream have dispersed.

I shade my eyes from the brightness of the sun as we approach the Castle. The glare makes it difficult to see anything but the general outlines of turrets, but I do hear singing and the sound of flutes. The rhythms bring goose bumps to my skin.

A familiar grey weathered cap atop the highest steeple catches my attention. His cloak ripples in the breeze making him look like a large faerie himself. Even from such a distance the glow in his eyes flash, even against the sparkle of the sun. I remember the first time I saw Laegaire, even before meeting Morici at Emerald Mountain. My heart flutters faster as I take in his warm gaze. Then I see the others beside him.

Culain. The Abbesses. Colin. Tears of joy flow effortlessly. They are safe. The Castle is safe. The Enchantment is saved!

They all begin to wave. Morici alights on Laegaire's staff. Ermanci flies to Culain's shoulder. Soon

Maeve gently drops me into their midst. The reunion is filled with hugs, tears, and a joy that tastes sweeter than any nectar. My friends look like angels to me. I feel like I am in heaven. An enchanting glow surrounds us with a wondrous blanket of rapture.

Laegaire wipes away my tears and his own. He kneels and holds my shoulders firmly but gently as though he is my father. My father! Some of the joy diminishes. The king and queen remain captured in Doe Castle. How can I forget them?

"Princess Deidre, you look pale." He pulls a salve from his pouch and rubs it on my cheeks. I feel them flush. I breathe more deeply. I feel Laegaire's care stir through me.

"I have been ill, but I am recovering."

Culain grabs my hands.

"I heard your flute. It gave me strength in the battle with Morgar."

This still sounds strange to me since I thought it was only a dream.

"I am just glad to be reunited with all of you."

Colin brings forth a small cup of some delicious honey mead.

"Partake, me lady, and ye will grow stronger."

The brew warms me in a way I had never felt before. I stand taller. I breathe deeper. Indeed, I feel my vitality returning.

"I love all of you! I missed you so." I hug the dark folds of Brigit's robes. Margaret strokes my hair like a loving aunt.

"We love you as well, dear princess. The combined love of all of us defeated Morgar." Then Morici shape-shifts into her human form, but her face and appearance glow. Her skin is richer. Her hair falls in long tresses rather than tangled masses. Her beauty is beginning to shine.

A tear in her eye sparkles like a rainbow in the sunlight. She lifts me in her arms and holds me like the sister that I never met. The warmth of her heart touches mine. She kisses me on my forehead.

"I am so glad you are safe. I apologize for the harm my father and I have brought to you and your parents. Please forgive me."

"I only feel love for you, Morici. How is your father?" As she puts me down and looks away, I sense her shame.

"He's not repentant. But his powers are gone thanks to Culain and the rest of us. And you. Maybe you can help him as you did me?" I look at Culain and wink. He smiles back with his own impish wink.

"I think it's Culain you should ask." She looks at him. He bows to her with a sweeping gesture.

"He is very angry at me right now, but I will make peace with him soon." Conviction exudes from Culain. Morici looks relieved.

An unexpected intruder barges into our reunion. It is a blackbird. One of Morici's. Blood drips from its beak. Its broken feathers make its flight jagged, as it almost hits the edge of the turret. Morici catches him in her arms.

"My messenger brings dark news. Brugh Donn has gathered a large force. They've taken St. Michael's and arrested all those staying there."

"All of them?" My heart goes out to Caleb and Martha. I look at Culain and wonder about Eamonn and Eldonna.

"All. And Fr. Malachy's in the dungeon. On the rack."

The breath almost goes out of me. How can they treat a priest of Patrick with such cruelty? I can only remember his kindness to me.

Maeve is right. Darkness still grips Eire.

"Any other news?"

Morici listens to the blackbird and gasps aloud. She covers her face with her hands.

"What is it?" Fear clamps on my heart.

"It's scheduled for tomorrow at noon."

"What! What's scheduled?" I taste the salty tears dripping onto my lips.

"The hanging of Conchubar and Macha."

I cannot see for my tears or hear over my cries as I hug Morici's skirts with all my might.

Chapter 12

To Save the King

s I open my eyes, Morici is holding me in her lap. *Laegaire brings a damp cloth to wipe my brow. The rest are gathered around me with wounded looks and sighs of relief that I am conscious. My fainting at the news of the noon hanging of the king and queen hit me like a sucker punch. My body already is weak from the rigors of the fever. The news sours the bright reunion with a dark pall. I look at the blackbird resting wobbly on Morici's shoulder. The ooze of blood from its chest is like the bleeding I feel inside. I see a hangmen's knot in my mind. I shiver more from the image than from the fever. The message is a dagger to my heart.*

"Deidre, fear not. Without Morgar, we can defeat

Brugh Donn!"

Culain's optimism brings a wan smile to my lips, but I know the real danger.

"If we attack, there'll be no hope for the king and queen, Culain."

The still silence confirms their begrudging agreement. Culain turns away and paces to the edge of the turret. The bright sun and the lush green view cannot lift the weight of silence. Margaret speaks.

"I have an idea!"

I had not heard much from Abbess Margaret before now, this earnest, quiet sister of Brigit. Angus had always said, "It's best for ye to listen when Margaret speaks, however infrequent that may be."

Brigit views her sister's eyes and a smile begins to emerge from her face as though the two exchanged ideas without the benefit of words. Margaret is as strong and tall as Brigit. She steps forward in worn robes and beads, standing to her full height and power.

"Tell them, sister Margaret. Tell them!"

"Morgar will save the king!" The silence claps hard around our ears. I can see only disbelief in all the eyes around me save the two sisters. My brief feeling of hope wilts like a flower in the desert. My head falls into

Morici's shoulder. Surely the abbesses have lost their minds. How can the Dark Enchanter who nearly destroyed the Enchantment be our savior?

Culain climbs up onto the very edge of the turret wall, making me gasp for his safety. His initial frown has yielded to an optimistic smile. Margaret's words have cast a spell over him. I wonder if everyone is losing their mind.

"Deidre and I will go as prisoners of Morgar! They will never suspect us." He flashes a confident look and extends his sword. But I think to myself, how can we possibly trust Morgar? As I search his eyes, I see a belief not only in Margaret's plan, but in his own confidence that he can convert Morgar as I helped Morici find her true heart. I begin to relate to that belief, but still I worry that these ideas reach too far with too much risk.

Laegaire gives the damp cloth to Morici and she wraps me in the folds of her robe. I simply hold her, too numb from all these swirling events to know what I feel.

"Culain, you and Margaret underestimate Morgar. He won't change as easily as Morici. He's steeped in darkness. Such an undertaking is far too risky for you and Deidre. If anyone goes with Morgar it will be me." Laegaire's courage is evident. With my weakness, I am drawn to the idea of Laegaire accompanying me. I trust his strength. While he stares at Culain, however, Margaret steps between them, separating them with the extension of her arms, looking as though she has wings.

"Nonsense, ye pompous men! I'll go with Deidre and Morgan. Brugh Donn trusts me. I am the abbess he knows. He knows ye not. It's Deidre that Brugh Donn wants. And it's Deidre that he'll get!"

The wind swirls around her skirts as she pulls out her own sword and holds it aloft and sparks fly from its tip. Margaret has spoken! Her wisdom spreads through us like mist covering a lake at dusk. She is not joking. Indeed, she knows Brugh Donn better than any of us. But does she know Morgar? Her conviction is beginning to convince me that her plan may have a chance to succeed.

Maeve flies beside Culain, lifting him down from the turret wall. Indeed, it is time for her wisdom and her magic to settle our thoughts and guide us. Her wings stir up a faery dust that sprinkles each of us with a graceful blessing. We all wait and listen.

"Only the highest level of enchantment can save the king and his queen from the hangman. Margaret speaks to the truth of the Enchantment. I trust her wisdom and send her with my blessing. It is time for us all to support her plan."

Morici and Brigit hold me tightly as they smile

from their depths. Brigit's pride in her sister glows. Despite my nagging doubts, I feel reassured by the love of these women.

Nacham flashes in front of me with a fearful look. I feel his concern for me with all the risks of this plan. I see in his eyes the unspoken words, "Is this folly?" but I raise a finger to my lips asking silence and open my arms to him for a gentle hug. I know Gabrielle is reminding me to trust my heart, a heart that trusts in Queen Maeve.

Brigit walks me over to Margaret and gently passes me into her arms. Margaret's smile warms me. An electric energy pulses through me. Maeve catches my eye with a supportive wink, as Brigit speaks.

"Take good care of this royal princess, dear sister, as I have these many years. It's time for her to save the king."

The words send a chill through me, a rapturous chill. Still, Nacham's voice refuses to be quiet. He whispers in my ear.

"Deidre, you've endured enough. How can this abbess protect you against the wiles of Morgar and Brugh Donn? Save yourself. The king and queen are already lost."

"Nacham, I won't abandon them. I can't. My

heart won't let me."

I need to act. "Margaret, please let me be free."

I step into the center of my friends.

"My courageous friends, I am weakened, but I'm not weak. I trust in the enchanting power in all of us. Now is the time to take heart. I'll be all right."

My words are full of my power, but my legs crumple beneath me. The ravages of fever, illness, and emotion are too much for my frame. The good Margaret catches me and I close my eyes and lean against her chest.

"My dear Deidre, rest now and listen to Maeve."

The queen of the faeries expands her wings to almost encircle the turret and all of us in it.

"Be aware of the dangers that we face. There's no room for error. Each one of ye must play yer role. Culain must convert Morgar to our plan. Laegaire, ye and Abbess Brigit must go to St. Michael's. Those who have cared for the princess and Culain are under house arrest. They need ye."

Then she turns to Morici.

"But ye, my dear Morici, must shape-shift back into a raven and be the eyes and ears for Margaret and Deidre. Take Ermanci with ye."

The former captain just about dances in the sky as he squawks and squeals with joy. Morici bids him quiet as she transforms into her bird-shape. Her wounded messenger has regained some strength and lands on Margaret's shoulder and tweaks at her ear. We all laugh.

Then Maeve approaches Margaret and me and strokes my cheek.

"Princess, ye are a brave daughter of the King, but ye are weak. Attend to the ministries of yer escorts. Remember all ye have learned in the Enchantment."

I smile weakly and consider her eyes.

"Are they still alive?"

"Yes, me child. Now it's time for rest before ye journey to Doe Castle."

Colin waves to us to follow him down the turret steps and Maeve rises and flies to the courtyard in a graceful glide. The three black flyers follow suit.

Laegaire looks at Culain.

"I guess this is one time that we must yield to the Queen." Culain smiles at his mentor.

"It won't be the last time."

I look sternly at both.

"It's not the Queen you yield to, it's the

Enchantment."

They both stop and look me in the eye and at each other. They pull out their swords and clash them gently, sending sparks aloft.

"Yes, Deidre. We yield to the Enchantment."

"Can you make Morgar yield, Culain?"

Laegaire speaks, sword still aloft and sparking, "It won't be Culain, dear Deidre. It'll be the Enchantment."

I smile broadly and Margaret giggles.

Despite our worry, we can still laugh.

It may just be Maeve's faerie dust, but I am grateful for a wee bit of levity.

Chapter 13

High Stakes

s Margaret lays me across the same bed I first slept on in the Faerie Castle, I succumb to a deep dreamless sleep. I recall the image of a vast still sea covered by a sheer clinging mist. I feel one with the waters and vapors. Still. Calm. At peace.

Suddenly the peace is broken by Culain's voice. The mists disperse and I stand upon what appears to be solid ground, back at the Castle. Somehow, I am transported into his presence, yet remain asleep in the bed.

I immediately sense that Culain struggles. He cannot see me, but my mind floats into his and I observe his state of mind through his own eyes as he begins to share his plight with me:

Deidre, I stand alone on the steps of the Sand Castle as I prepare to meet Morgar. I still

bristle at Margaret's "pompous" remark. I can
defend you, Deidre. I can defeat Brugh Donn!
I have great confidence in my ability to wield the
powerful energy of the Enchantment.

"But it's not about winning, Culain."
Gabrielle always gets my attention as she lands
on my right shoulder and brushes her wings
across my ear. As usual she is right! I just
don't always like to listen. She has my
attention. I pat her white feathers.

But dark feathers appear on my left
shoulder and Nog (much like your own
Nacham, Deidre), chimes in his question.

"What does Gabrielle know that you
don't? Follow your logic and reason! Trust in
your ability to win battles!" I yearn to listen to
him over Gabrielle, but I want to follow the true
path.

"Gabrielle, am I not supposed to use the
sword skills Lugh taught me?"

"There's a time and place for that. Not
now. Now is the time to focus on helping
Morgar understand the true beauty of
Enchantment."

"But if he just pretends to understand who will defend Margaret and Deidre?"

Nog cheers my question, jumping up and down on my left shoulder. I see him more visibly for the first time in a while. Some of his brown feathers trickle to the ground.

Gabrielle, luminescent and snow white, flies in front of me. Her visage mesmerizes me. Even Nog pulls in his wings and sits quietly on my shoulder.

"Culain, if you can't trust in the power of Enchantment, how will you ever convince Morgar? Your task isn't to fight now, it's to let the Enchantment energies transform you and Morgar."

"But what if I fail? What if he deceives me?"

"If you listen to your heart, deception is impossible." Nog stands up on my shoulder and whispers in my ear.

"I hate to admit it, but she's making sense." His breath tickles me and I rub my ear and nearly knock him down, but he holds his perch.

I pace nervously. I want to engage Brugh Donn and his men with my sword. Gabrielle hears my thoughts.

"Engaging Brugh Donn will be the death of the King!" Nog flies in front of me and nods his agreement. Ganging up on me! I know it is time for me to yield. If I cannot trust in the power of the heart, how can I ever convince Morgar? It is not about waging battles. It is about winning hearts.

"Enough of debate, Gabrielle and Nog. Leave me alone now, so that I can gather myself for Morgar."

My two trusted faeries fly out of view and I sit alone on the steps. Then I spot a small oak tree near the bottom. I did not see it before. I am drawn to it and walk over to wee tree.

"Take me leaf!"

"What?"

"Ye heard me!" Even these little oaks can be obstinate.

"Okay!" I grab one of the smaller leaves. It feels fresh, almost wet with dew.

It veins are rich with green.

"Now chew!"

"Wait a minute now." The little tree shakes and brushes its tiny branches across my shins.

"No minutes left. Now!" The wee tree shakes more violently until some of its other leaves begin to fall off.

"Okay!" I put the leaf in my mouth. It is bitter. Oaks are bitter. But I chew and the little oak stands still. I hear a chuckle.

"How do ye feel?" I am ready to spit out the concoction and grimace accordingly, but I do feel a tingling in my mouth.

"Spit it out now. Ye're ready." I sure am, but the tingling spreads to my whole body. It soothes pleasantly.

"The enchantment of Oak now fills you, Culain of Eire!" Movement stops and silence prevails.

I pat the wee oak, and, as I try to leave, my feet root solidly into the earth. I try lifting them, but they are stuck. I untie my shoes, but the laces retie each time. These leprechaun shoes have a mind of their own!

I sit down on the ground next to the infant tree.

"I give up, wee oak. What do I do next?"

"I am no wee oak, lad! I am the seed of Ankara. His life is in me veins. And now it runs in ye." The name of Ankara stirs my heart. The voice echoes Ankara's trademark tone. I smile at his repartee.

"Do I have to stay here forever, Ankara?"

"What sort of fool do ye take us for, lad! Just call out her name."

"Who?"

"The one ye asked to leave ye alone." I feel a chill run down to my roots. I looked about and whisper.

"G....Ga......Gabrielle?"

I feel a tugging at my ankle. Looking down, I hear her giggle. She drops faerie dust on my shoes. Then I hear Lugh's pipe and begin to dance. The roots are set free. As the freed feet settle down, I walk back to the wee Oak.

"Thanks, Ankara."

I hear no reply, but receive the gentlest bow.

I turn to Gabrielle and stare into her eyes, deep pools of endless turquoise. I hold her tiny hand in mine as I look, silently, as though looking at eternity. I feel a calmness that settles me. The urgency to act alone, to be right, to attack — all fades like a gentle mist.

"Culain, the wisdom of Oak now runs in your veins and fills your heart. Be one with the Oak. Go now to Morgar -- without judgement, and with love."

I feel her hand release me and watch her fly up to the tree branches until her image fades away. Nog lands on my shoulder and whispers in my ear.

"Our only chance is for you to make Morgar our ally. Can you do it?"

"It won't be me, Nog, it will be all of us through the common flow of Enchantment."

Nog nods. And gives a gentle nip on my earlobe.

"Good luck, Culain. It's time for me to leave you to your destiny."

As the leaves blend around his departing wings, I turn toward the Castle steps. Morgar is in the small dining room where Deidre and I re-united after our trials. As I enter the room, guarded only by Colin, Morgar paces about the grey stone block floor, ignoring the luscious food on the table. He looks remorseless. Were there a fireplace in his head, the flames and smoke would be roaring out his mouth and ears. He glares at me.

"Ye cursed child, Culain! How dare ye challenge me skills!" He makes all the motions of a court enchanter -- waving arms, billowing dust, squinting eyes. But nothing happens. I pick up an apple, bite crisply, and begin to savor its enchanting sweetness.

I grabbed a peach and throw it at him. He catches it easily.

"Morgar, rest your energies for now. The Greater Enchantment prevails here. Your powers can be restored — if you come to your senses."

As the peach roars past my ear and splats its sticky orange contents upon the wall, I smile at my adversary.

"These peaches are from an enchanted orchard, Morgar. Try it again."

The peach reforms its shape and flies into my hand. As I throw it to him again, I take out my sword and lay it upon the food table.

"You can take the sword as well."

He drops the peach and rushes to the flashing brilliance of the lustrous metal. Its power beguiles this dark wizard of a man. He lifts it and brandishes it with delight and chuckles with a condescending laugh.

"This cockiness of yers will be yer

undoing, boy!" He thrusts the point directly into my belly area. I feel totally calm as I watch the hilt reach my navel. The mists billow from the sword and then envelop us entirely. No peaches. No apples. No tables. No sign of Colin.

When I see his face again, Morgar is only about 5 years old, a bright-eyed boy with tears at the corners of his eyes. As I look closer, I recognize the face. It is mine. I blink and pinch myself, but there I am. And Morgar, or I, or whoever, is holding the hilt of the sword in his hand.

He drops the hilt and looks at me, eye to eye. For minutes, or hours, or years, or millenniums. I do not know, for time has no meaning. At first, I see old fears, angers, and his need to control clinging to his thoughts, but the Enchantment begins to melt these icy parts of his mind, to help him get in touch with his inner self, his heart. Once he crosses that threshold, his eyes transform. All that is left is a growing love, peace, and joy that had not been allowed to shine. It beguiles me, nurtures me and comforts me. I stretch my open hand to him.

"Morgar, let us return to time and embrace love. The core of your heart calls you to me, to Deidre, and to Morici. We need your help with Brugh Donn when the mists disperse. I offer you my hand in friendship."

His gaze returns the answer as does the gentle grasp of his hand. I feel an electric charge pass through us, a lightning-like jolt. He smiles and hands me a leaf, an oak leaf.

"My heart is with you, Culain. Let us return."

The mist disappears and we find ourselves flat on our backs on the floor of the dining room. The sword lies between us. Morgar begins to reach for the sword, but I throw the peach toward him. He catches it instead and gives it a generous bite and sweet peach nectar oozes down the sides of his mouth.

"Sweet, Culain, very sweet!" He picks up an apple knocked to the floor and throws it at me. I catch it easily and take an equally big crunch. Its nectar is like ambrosia.

Then Morgar grabs the sword and runs toward me. He strikes the sword powerfully into the wooden floor between my legs and holds the hilt. I stand up and put my hands around his and behold his eyes.

"For the Enchantment of All!" The same words came forth spontaneously from each of us.

Colin comes over and puts a hand on each of our shoulders.

"Margaret, Morgar is ready!"

Chapter 14

To Church

Culain continues to Deidre...

rigit and Margaret nearly trip over each other as they burst through the door, their skirts and beads all askew. As our laughter rises, each abbess takes a position behind a member of our new alliance. I can feel Margaret's strong hands sink into my shoulders and knead them gently. Brigit does the same for Morgar. The gentle sweet energy of the alliance surges among us.

Margaret speaks to Morgar's softened visage. "Have you rejoined the Enchantment of

All?"

He raises one arm in the manner of an oath, "I proclaim my allegiance to The Enchantment!" His wide smile and extended arm confirm the veracity of his words. As much as such a change seemed so unlikely, I believe him.

Brigit adds, "Culain of Eire, do you affirm Morgar and pass to him the care of Margaret and Deidre before Brugh Donn at Doe Castle?"

I raise my hand in oath, "I affirm Morgar and pass to him the care of Margaret and Deidre in the name of The Enchantment of All." My voice surges at the end as if part of the cadence of a march. I have no doubts, Deidre. Nothing is ever certain, but I believe you can trust him.

I feel a tingling pass through all of us, so that the hair on my arms stands on end. I feel the energy of Morgar's heart as his hands and mine continue to grasp Lugh's sword. Colin grabs firmly upon our arms.

"Morgar of Spain and Culain of Eire, you have chosen your missions. May the full force of The Enchantment carry you on your journeys."

Then the flutter of great wings catches our attention. Queen Maeve hovers over us.

"The time is upon us. Brugh Donn's hangmen have erected their towers. Morgar, you must use all your skill and guile as you carry Deidre to Doe castle. Listen carefully to Margaret's words."

Morgar releases the hilt of the sword and moves quickly toward the door.

"Wait, Morgar!" I pull out the sword, grab it by the blade and extend the hilt to him.

"You may need this." He bows, takes the sword, and raises it aloft.

"For the Enchantment of All!" He rushes out.

The Faerie Queen's voice chimes for me. "Culain, the villagers of St. Michael's including your foster parents and Deidre's are under guard in the church. Laegaire, Brigit and Colin will assist you in freeing them, so no harm comes to them."

"My Queen, what of Fr. Malachy?" Her face falls and her voice drops.

"He's at Doe Castle on the dungeon rack." We gasp in disbelief.

"So, my friends, ye must free the villagers and then meet Margaret, Morgar and the princess to see if ye can save Fr. Malachy. Use the Oval Gate to speed your travel to Ulster."

She needs say no more. We fly through the door as if we have wings. Queen Maeve's real wings lift her out the window with the grace of a swan. I pray that she is heading to Doe Castle to assist your quest there, Deidre.

Laegaire meets us by the steps, with the reins of fresh steeds in his hands. I pray for the safety of Morgar and Margaret, but climb my mount rapidly. I want to wish you luck in your mission, dear Deidre, and hope that your recovery is strengthening you. But there is no time now for a farewell as I have my own quest to attend. I must be off!

I feel the rippling muscles of the fine animal beneath my legs. The power of this horse soon sweeps me forward along the trail.

Laegaire knows the shorter path to the Oval Gate that Maeve recommended — a broader portal where our band can cross from the Enchantment back to Ulster and St. Michaels. The River Veritas runs through it. As we go through a misty circular opening in the forest, the rush of fog dims my vision. The barrier between worlds is thinner here. This may be the gate Morgar breached to enter the Enchantment in the first place. The horses can ride through without falling through a cavern. My steed does whinny and rises as we pass through, but I can hold tight. I can barely see the current of Veritas beside us as it is covered thickly with cloudy vapors.

As the mists lift while we ride again on the familiar grey roads of Ulster, I pick up speed. I can barely see the others behind me from the storm of dust in our wake. I need not spur my mount forward. I simply hold close so that the wind sweeps over me as though I am one with the steed.

As we approach St. Michael's church, I see hawks perched in the surrounding trees. I reach for my sword. Then I remember two things. The sword is with Morgar and the hawks are on his side — now OUR side as well! I smile and raise my arm as if it is a sword. Sparks fly from my fingertips and light the sky. Hawks stir and circle the church steeple. Several predators fly toward me. I tell the others to fear not. One hawk lands gracefully on each of our shoulders as our horses approach the steps of St. Michaels. They now are guardians, not tormentors. An enchanting change!

Darkness, however, still grips Brugh Donn's soldiers. The ice-girded henchmen guarding the steps of St. Michael's barely have slits open in their eyes. Two men who hold Eldonna between them with a sword to her throat shout out a warning to us.

"Engage us and yer friends die instantly!"

Laegaire, Brigit, Colin and I dismount but back away with a warning from Brigit:

"Listen to them, Culain. They've taken Fr. Malachy to the Doe Castle dungeon."

A soldier slaps Eldonna's cheek so sharply with his coarse hand that it draws blood. Brigit's words hold me back, but the hawks do not deter. Several birds fly directly at the attacking soldier. The armored brute backs away from the screeching birds with extended talons. Then the other hawks join in swiftly as the soldiers draw Eldonna behind the church doors. Some birds slip in the crack of the door opening. Others fly through the belfry. Before long, the soldiers come bursting out the doors as talons cut the flesh of their arms and faces. They leave the villagers behind, and run down the street. We let them pass, but two towering guards appear at the door, one with Eldonna and the other with Martha. The points of their swords nick slits of blood from the women's necks. Again, we back away.

"Take me, instead, soldiers of Brugh Donn." I feel no fear. These soldiers have so much ice on them that the hawks cannot penetrate their skin. The leader sees the opportunity.

"It's Sultain's son! He'll be a great prize!"

They grab me gruffly as Laegaire, Brigit and Colin hold their ground and accept Martha and Eldonna into their protection.

Laegaire raises his staff. The soldiers stop. "This is your final warning. Release the boy!" He sends a bolt of lightning to the steeple, felling stones to the ground next to us.

"Foolish old buzzard, ye will not harm us or the lad will die! Stand down!"

I feel a cold prick of metal at my throat, but do not flinch. I need a diversion. On cue, I see the flapping of brown wings. It is Nog. I thought he had remained in the Enchanted Forest, but he flies at the soldier holding me. The blade leaves my neck and flails at Nog. My faerie dodges the thrust, but his tail feathers fall to the ground and his flight turns drunken.

"Help me!" I cry to no one.

Caleb emerges from behind us and grabs the larger soldier around the throat, pulling him to the ground. I struggle free, but the other soldier grabs my tunic and pulls me to him, tearing the cloth.

Laegaire's sword clangs upon the soldier's icy breastplate and the guard falls to the ground like timber, taking me down with him. His foul smell envelopes me and the icy sharpness of his armor digs into my chest as he rolls on top of me.

"Lugh, help me!" I call out. I feel a fire burn in my hands. It surges into the soldier's armor, melting ice and metal and I roll the beast of a man off me and sizzling ice vaporizes into a cloud of steam. As I continue to hold his breastplate, heat sears from my hands and brings a roar from the man. He flees down the street. Brigit and Colin aid Caleb in subduing the remaining soldier.

Eamonn emerges and embraces his wife Eldonna as tears mix with the blood on his face from the brutality of the soldiers. Brigit strides over to them to tend their wounds. My memories of their cruelty to me melt into the breeze and I run to Brigit's arms that beckon me to join in a hug with her and my battered family. I help her in placing green balm and faerie dust upon their bruises.

Eamonn kneels as scarlet streaks still ooze from his face and he holds me by the shoulders. New tears soften the streaks to pink.

"Me son, I am so sorry we failed ye so

often."

I place my hand upon his heart and look directly into his eyes.

"You only strengthened me the more, Da, to prepare me for my destiny. You tested the depth of my love to make it even stronger. And I do love you, Da. I'm sorry I ran away without telling you."

I feel the warmth pulsing down my hand to Da's heart. Despite all his failings, at the core of his heart, he loves me.

Brigit puts a hand to my shoulder.

"I knew Eamonn and Eldonna would test you and strengthen you, Culain. That's why I put you in their care."

I grasp Brigit's hand and feel the sweet warmth.

Mum strokes my face, brushing the long locks to the side. She considers my eyes.

"I, too, am sorry for me ways with drink, Culain. The good Brigit knew our weakness, but she knew that we would always love ye. Ye are so brave, me son. I do love ye so much."

She embraces me with an unfamiliar warmth. Tears roll onto her tunic. I hug her warmly.

When I look up I see Martha and Caleb. They each hold out a stone for me.

"Culain, these stones are quartz, feldspar, and granite. Lugh told us they were for you and Deidre. One of each type for both of you. He said that you would know what to do with them."

The stones of the Birch, Rowan, and Oak moons almost vibrated. Their rich energy would strengthen and support us. I feel them almost sizzle in my palm.

"Thank you, I'll take them to her."

I hug the innkeepers and I know, Deidre, that you will be proud of their renewed love for you, especially Caleb's heroism in saving me. Lugh trusts them, so should we.

Laegaire's staff stands firm in the distance, his robes flying up in a gust of wind. His eyes hold the fiery zeal I knew forever. Colin walks up to me and extends his hand to shake mine.

"Time's fleeting, me friend. King

Conchubar needs us now. Deidre needs us. We must go before it's too late."

I raise my arm over my head.

"To Doe Castle, my friends!"

"May the Enchantment fill you!" The words came from above the church steeple. It is the voice of Lugh. He winks at me. As I stride for my steed, I hear his flute play with verve and gusto.

Dust and hooves become my companions again as Brigit, Laegaire, and Colin each ride to one side of me -- left, right, and rear. At the Oval Gate, the mists spread like a curtain, as though it knows that we must not delay. The refreshing waters of Veritas flow beside us. We rush onward into the Enchantment, bearing down the road to the Faerie Castle.

As the castle turrets come into view, my heart sinks. Dark, foreboding clouds hang like lead painted across the sky. Nog whispers into my ear, "We're too late! We're too late!"

Chapter 15

The Oval Gate

Deidre continues:

 s I awaken from my healing sleep in the Enchanted Sand Castle, eyes still shut, I recall the dream revelations that Culain has already left with Laegaire and others to save our friends at St. Michael's. My mind whirls, wondering if these dreams are true. My hands twitch and clench the covers as my eyes remain closed, uncertain if I am awakened or still in a dream. Has Morgar indeed become an ally? Has Culain succeeded or will Morgar revert to his old dark, cold ways? Fear rises in me making my heart race and perspiration glistens on my brow. Can we trust Morgar to help us to stay the gallows intended for my true parents, High King Conchubar, and his Queen Macha? Still groggy from the magical sleep, eyes barely open, I blurt out:

"Margaret! Where are you?"

"Relax, my child." Margaret intones quietly as she sits on the edge of the bed and begins to caress my forehead, wiping away the thin film of moisture. Her touch calms me, but my eyelids seem too heavy to open.

"Our friends are safe with the Champion of Ulster. Take some deep breaths."

She sprinkles some unfamiliar fairy dust over my eyes to open them fully. Her warm face and gentle smile soften my fear. Her touch is gentle and reassuring. I put my hand on hers.

"Can we save them, Margaret?"

"My dear child, Culain has touched Morgar's heart as you did with Morici. We have a plan, an enchanted plan that will work. Arise now, it is time to go. Your healing is complete. Culain has shared our plan with you in your dream."

I wonder how she knows about my dream, but she is on the mark! I know the plan. I know her role. I know Morgar's role. The Enchantment is indeed amazing.

I am surprised at how strong I feel after battling with fever and a badly bruised forehead. I feel for the lump there. It is gone. Margaret sees my discoveries and winks.

"You indeed are ready. Morgar and the horses are waiting for you." She gives me a wet towel to wash my face and a cup of the finest spring water I have ever tasted. And a peach, a lovely peach! I bite into it. I will need my strength. I remember the peaches of the dream. I smile to myself at the magic fruit.

"Thank you, Margaret." I give her a warm hug.

"My dear Deidre, we will be taking the same path that Laegaire and Culain took to cross the realm of Enchantment into Eire. It is the Oval Gate, guarded by Oaks. It will shorten our time to Doe Castle. Fear not, my child. A spell of Enchantment has been cast and the blessing of saints and archangels are upon us."

Then she adds, with a wink, "And I know how to handle Brugh Donn. He may be greedy and cruel, but he is just a man like any other."

Her words hearten me. I feel stronger. I recall the Oval Gate from the dream. I look forward to seeing it in person. Yet another reminder that what I saw through Culain's eyes in my dream was not imaginary.

Once we start riding, doubts still linger in me about Morgar. As I observe him upon his horse, I no longer see the icy crust around his face or his heart. I wonder, though, will they return, once we arrive at the castle? This is the same Morgar that captured the beloved

Faerie Sand Castle in very heart of the Enchantment!

As if he heard my thoughts, Morgar looks at me solemnly.

"Forgive me, Princess Deidre. I was blinded by power and greed. But Culain has changed me." Without waiting for a response, he charges ahead as we reach the Oval Gate.

As he nears an Oak, its branch strikes him to the ground.

"Ye deceived us once, Morgar. Not again! Ye shall not pass the Oval Gate!" It is as though both Ankara and Osiris are speaking as one.

I dismount and grab Morgar's hand and help him up.

I walk over to the Great Oak and hug him.

"My dearest Oaks, Ankara and Osiris, our own Faerie Queen Maeve has commissioned us to leave. To save the King. To save the Queen. The Champion Culain has touched Morgar's heart. We must allow him to take us through the Oval Gate."

Surprisingly there is no biting response, no rebuke. Only a flourish of a tree branch, bidding us to go ahead.

I curtsey. "Thank you, great Ankara and Osiris!"

I climb back onto my horse. Morgar dusts himself off and remounts his steed with a tip of his hat in thanks to me and to the Oaks. They shake their branches at him with a final flourish as a warning for him to fulfill his duty. Morgar speeds ahead, slightly rattled. I cover my smile at these impish proud Oaks.

The misty shield of the Oval Gate clears and we ride through, waving to the Oaks.

I pray that my speech to the Oaks about Morgar is on the mark. The lives of my parents are depending on it. Margaret flashes me a reassuring smile and I take a deep breath.

As we travel on in silence, Doe Castle comes into view ahead.

Morgar leads us with the plan to make the ruse that Margaret and I are his captives. Or is it a ruse? Older icy fears rise in me. Frost forms on my chest. I know that I trust Morici with my life, but this is the same Morgar that Morici battled with such zeal and with such failure. Margaret said Morici and Ermanci would meet us at Doe Castle, but I have not seen them yet. Are they flying above?

I detect a suddenly venomous look in Morgar's eyes. I trust Culain and the abbesses implicitly, but part of me wonders if they have gone mad after all. Is this not the Darkest of Dark Enchanters? Then I hear Gabrielle whisper in my ear, even though I do not see her.

"Deidre, isn't this the father of Morici? Don't you know her heart as yours?"

The warmth returns to my chest and my heart beats more calmly. I watch Margaret hold herself with such dignity and strength in the saddle. The same fire burns in her eyes that I saw in Laegaire's. Truly she is the same blood as Brigit. She turns and winks at me, allaying any vestiges of fear. But now we close in to Doe Castle! The blackness of clouds gives me an icy chill. The air temperature plunges. The wind rises. I begin to worry about my true father, the true King, Conchubar. And my true mother, the Queen Macha. A tear rises in the corner of my eye. It feels hard as though it already is frozen.

Margaret rides close to me to me and wipes the tear away.

"Trust in the Enchantment." She guides in a whisper. Her touch is reassuring. But the cold makes me shiver. We approach a place where darkness is so real I can almost taste its bitterness and smell its acrid odor.

As we near the moat, Morgar digs his heels into his mount and it rears up on its rear legs and neighs loudly. The enchanter holds his mount firmly, but the noise catches the attention of the gatekeeper.

"Lower the gate, fool!" Is Morgar just pretending to be his old self, I wonder, or are we the fools?

"Be quick about it, you idiot! Can't you see I have the princess?" He looks at me with a sneer and grabs me roughly about the neck, shaking me.

My eyes water and I call out, "Margaret!"

I never saw an arm move more quickly, but before I know it Margaret swats his hand from my neck and throws Morgar to the ground. His mount storms away.

"You cursed woman, how dare you test me!" Then the gate groans and falls to the ground with such a crash I thought it would shatter into splinters. Morgar redirects his anger to the gatekeeper.

"Idiot, I'll have your skin for such incompetence!"

He grabs the reins to my horse and leads me forward. Margaret rides astride him.

"If you touch that girl again, you will be in the moat!"

Morgar raises his arms and begins to get that electric look in his eyes as though he is going to send a bolt of lightning toward her, but her look alone admonishes him and he curses under his breath. My heart is pounding as I look for help. Morici and Ermanci finally appear. One lands on Margaret's shoulder. The other lands on Morgar's and gives him a little peck on the cheek. He shoos Morici away and she flies to my shoulder. I feel calmer knowing allies have arrived. I also grab the hilt of my sword. Its warmth comforts me. Margaret grips hers as well.

As we enter, the darkness behind the gate is so thick that I can barely see through it. The afternoon looks almost like midnight under a pale moon. Ice-bound guards mill around or pound on wood in the distance. As horses walk across the bridge, a chilling sight emerges.

The scaffold is tall and sturdy, built of fresh hewn wood. I feel sorry for the tree that gave its life for this purpose. I see a circular noose dangling from the beam above the trap door. Hammers pound final braces. Hanging is imminent. My heart rises in my throat and tears fill my eyes, so that all becomes a blur. Margaret pats my shoulder.

"Be strong, Deidre. Trust."

Morici strokes my cheek with her feathers. I relish her presence and her support, but the fear gives me a shiver that frosts my chest and my eyebrows.

The clang of armor echoes as the icy entourage of Brugh Donn's troops march forward, and a tall thick-necked man with a scowl shouts out.

"Morgar, ye have the princess. Ha, ha, ha! We'll have a triple hanging. Guards, take this cleric woman to the dungeon to join Fr. Malachy."

Morgar raises his hand to stop them.

"Lord Brugh Donn, keep the woman here so she can see the folly of any resistance and tell her compatriots."

"Good idea, Morgar! Ye get cleverer with time. The hanging will commence at noon, when we hear the church steeple ring."

At these words, Ermanci flies off toward the church.

"It'll only be minutes before we're rid of the Conalls forever. Every one of them will finally be dispatched and the Donns will prevail."

I shake like a leaf in the wind. I hope that reinforcements are coming from the church. Is all lost? Has Morgar duped us? We are no match for these troops. I hang my head low. A guard snatches me from my horse and I do not resist. Margaret dismounts, shoves the guard aside and takes my hand as we walk in front of the scaffold.

"Feisty old cleric, isn't she, Morgar?" laughs Brugh Donn with a sour roar.

"She'll soon learn her lesson." Morgar glares at us. I look up at Margaret, but she is unafraid, as confident and proud as when we began our ride. It gives me strength and I follow her manner and feel for the hilt of my sword.

Three dozen guards mill about the courtyard around the scaffold. They give us cold stares but otherwise leave us alone. They pay more attention to Brugh Donn, who metes out orders. Two guards flank us on either side, huge men covered with icy chests and threatening spears. Any attempts to escape clearly will be a mistake. All we can do is wait. A new group of men enter the courtyard, arguing in loud voices.

I gasp at the familiar visage of my father, the High King, standing among them below the scaffold. A half-dozen guards restrain him as his voice rises. His face remains free of ice. Fire rages in his eyes. He struggles and roars at the guards. I am both impressed by his vigor and fearful— for his life, for my life, for Queen Mum's life.

"Don't ye know that I was appointed High King at Tara itself? Fergus, don't ye remember the day? I trusted ye and now ye give allegiance to the Donns."

Fergus ignores him as the others constrain my father, but the plea continues.

"Brugh Donn is an imposter to the throne. He can't bear the mistakes of his ancestors and he blames me for their fall from power. But he alone is to blame. It's time to resist him."

The king's charges meet deaf ears and dark eyes. Even his trusted Fergus will not acknowledge his words. Brugh Donn has hardened their hearts. Ice covers their chests, their ears and their eyes. I wonder how they walk without tripping.

Then father's gaze finds me and our eyes meet.

"Deidre! Deidre!" He knocks down the two guards between us and runs to me. The two guards beside me try to intervene but Margaret trips them. He lifts me up and hugs me. I feel so warm in his arms. His face is a blur for the tears that fill my eyes.

I hear the clamor of metal and ice around me. I think for sure that our lives will end here and now from their swords. I prepare to die in the arms of my father. Will it not be better than hanging?

"Leave them be!" Brugh Donn's command is sharp and firm. The guards pull back.

"I won't give them the pleasure of the sword. They'll fall soon enough."

Chapter 16

Return of the King

egardless of what might happen, I am content to be held by my father and breathe in his presence. He kisses me on the forehead and runs his fingers through my hair. I feel like an angel. His ruddy color is full and rich and his eyes burn with love for me. I might as well be in heaven.

The Queen catches my attention. A single guard escorts her next to the gallows. Her head is downcast. The ice has returned to her face. I can almost feel her cold sorrow as if it is mine. She looks at us but does not see. She appears defeated, resigned, as though she already is hanged. Father sees what I see and turns my face to his.

"Deidre, I couldn't keep her with me since ye left.

The vapors have returned to her. Her sadness imprisons her spirit."

Margaret walks over to her as guards part. She brushes her hair and lifts her chin.

"My Queen, don't despair. The power of the Enchantment can never be extinguished." She places her hands on my mother's cheeks and the ice melts slowly, in drips. Small pieces fall to the ground. Her eyes catch Margaret's and she offers a weak smile.

"Is it ye, Margaret?"

"Yes, my Queen. And your husband holds your daughter. Come to her."

"Ye jest, Margaret, I don't see her."

She leads Macha to us. She looks at me blankly at first, as though I am a stranger. I reach out and touch the remaining ice upon her face. As it melts, her eyes open wider.

"Deidre? Is it ye, dearest?" Her eyes nearly plead with me to say yes.

I nod ever so softly. Tears pour forth and she clenches me to her, sobbing uncontrollably. I feel her warmth, but also her weakness and fear.

Father and Margaret join in the hugging and tears

pour freely from us all. Warm tears. Tears that continue to melt my mother's ice, bit by bit, until chunks begin to scatter about the ground.

"I love you, queen mum!" I squeeze her hand and behold her opening eyes. She smiles back at me weakly. "I....I....love ye too, my princess." Still she continues to sob. I hold her hand tightly and the king wraps her shoulders with his strong arm.

Then I feel an icy presence. The brash crusty armor of Brugh Donn spews its icy coldness enough to make me see my breath. He is holding his hands on his hips with a wide smile and a condescending laugh.

"So, this is royalty, eh? A bunch of sniveling cowards, all ye. We'll put ye out of yer misery soon, won't we, Morgar?"

Morgar stands in the gallows' shadows and says nothing. Does he feel any guilt at deceiving us? Is that why he stands back?

The King steps forward.

"Brugh Donn, ye may have quarrel with me, but ye have none with me wife and daughter. Hang me if ye will, but release them. Only a true coward kills women and children."

Brugh Donn bellows a deep laugh. "I need no

heirs of yers to bring the Conall blood alive again. We execute all three of ye when the noon bell rings."

Conchubar rushes forward and throws Brugh Donn to the ground with the tenacity of a tiger unleashed. He squeezes tightly about his neck. It is only moments before a half-dozen guards manhandle my father, bloodying his forehead and stabbing his shoulder. They hold him as Brugh Donn regains his footing, tottering at first. He draws out his sword to strike, but a hand rises to restrain him. It is Morgar's.

"Contain your anger, my liege! Don't make him a martyr to your sword. Let the rule of the courts execute him by hanging as we planned. A martyr's ghost can be more powerful than a man alive. Put down your sword!"

The rebel ruler puts away his sword in a huff, but he turns back to the High King.

"Ye and yer Conalls will pay in blood." Then he strikes Conchubar with the hilt of his sword, knocking him to the ground unconscious as blood pours from his face. Margaret kneels quickly beside him to treat the wound.

I scream "Stop!" but tears blur my eyes and I fall to the ground with sobs as queen mum follows me. The violence to our king shakes us to the core. Ice begins to form around both our faces as the tears turn blue white in their frozenness. Someone picks me up, but I don't care who it is.

"Be strong little one, reinforcements are near." I consider the face of Morici. She has shape-shifted into human form.

"Ermanci has put a stop to the bell. Hold still!"

No one seems to notice this new player. My heart quickens, my tears stop, and ice falls from my face. I grab the hilt of Lugh's sword. It is warm to the touch, almost hot.

I quickly search for my mother. Morgar is carrying her up to the top of the scaffolding. Would they dare to hang her first? I feel a fiery rage rise within me, but Morici whispers for quiet.

"Fear not, my princess. The Enchantment holds us safe." I choose to believe her and look about for the reinforcements but see none.

Then she puts three stones into my palm. One quartz. Another feldspar. The last granite. Their warmth glows in my hand.

"These are gifts from Martha and Caleb." I almost choke on my surprise.

"How did you get them?"

"From Culain."

"Where?"

"Shh!

I look about for a sign. The gallows executioner is checking the trap door. It trips with a loud bang. I look up and see two guards assist the dazed king up the gallows' stairs. Margaret is under Conchubar's left arm, holding the bandage to his face. I push forward to help them, but Morici holds me back. She points to the drawbridge chains. A shape-shifted Ermanci strikes them with the mighty blow of an ax. Morici's daytime shape-shifting magic now is Ermanci's as well. The Enchantment is helping us.

Nothing moves on the drawbridge despite several strikes from the seven-foot Spanish pirate, but the sound draws guards to his direction, shouting, "Seize him!"

The ax strikes again with a loud clang.

Still nothing moves. The guards are closing in on Ermanci. He glares at them.

A hand tugs on my shoulder. I see a fiery look in Morici's eyes. A lightning bolt flies out, striking the chain and dropping the drawbridge with a horrendous thud. Wooden planks splinter and spray this time, but enough remain for Laegaire to lead the charge into the castle. Reinforcements!

The dark outlines of Culain, Colin, and Brigit cast long shadows. Their swords burn bright. Ermanci engages his pursuers, driving back clanging blows with the zest of a pirate.

A dark figure scales the scaffold of the gallows. Brugh Donn is climbing the steps toward my father. His sword waves like sickle to wheat.

"Morgar won't stop me this time!"

"I beg to differ!" Morgar holds Culain's sword on the deck of the scaffold, ready for Brugh Donn. I would recognize the sword anywhere. Sparks fly from its tip like a Chinese sparkler. Brugh Donn's sword lunges toward the king anyway, but Morgar foils every strike. One guard grabs Morgar from behind, but as Brugh Donn's sword is about to strike him, the rebel king begins to sink. Father holds the hangman in his grip as he releases the trap door beneath Brugh Donn, who falls to the ground with a wail that stops at impact. The fallen usurper king does not move.

Most of the guards are engaged in combat with my friends, especially Morici's bolts. The magical powers of Morici and the enchantment of Lugh's swords overwhelm them like a tsunami. Soldiers run out on the drawbridge only to fall into the moat. Others run into the bowels of the castle screaming. Morici's lightning bolts topple towers and open gaping holes in walls. Steam sizzles from strikes by Laegaire, Culain, Brigit, and Colin. Fight burns in me, but Morici waves me up the steps of the scaffold while she directs her bolts of fire.

Morgar's sword has just penetrated the ice of the final soldier and rolls him off the side of the scaffold. My true Da rests with queen mum on the scaffold floor. Margaret tenderly wipes his face and beckons me with her arm. The waterfall of tears begins again as I embrace them.

Culain clamors up the steps. Morgar rushes to him.

"I have something to return to you, Culain." Morgar holds the blade of Lugh as he presents the hilt to its rightful owner.

"Well done, Morgar! I knew you could do it." I wish I had felt the same earlier. The trials Culain puts me through challenge me, but I forget them all in this redeeming moment. I run to Culain and hug him warmly. I see the scars on his cheek.

"How did you fight without your sword?" He extends his arm with black powder burns.

"It works without the blade, my friend." As he extends his arm, sparks fly from his palm. He laughs aloud and kisses me on the forehead. He kneels in front of me and extends his sword to me.

"My sword is at your service, my princess."

"Enough chivalry, Culain. Get up and meet my mum and da."

I turn to them and announce, "This is my good friend Culain, the new Champion of Ulster. He has saved us."

They embrace him as though he were their own son.

I love Culain, as though he is my brother. In my heart, I say, "Thank you for your courage, your strength, and your love."

The bells of St. Michael's ring in the distance, celebrating the return of the king.

Lugh's flute music dances in the air.

Chapter 17

Darkness Prevails

s *vapors of melting ice waft over the courtyard, Brigit limps towards us up the steps of the scaffold, sword in hand.* Her *white robes bear patches of mud and a crimson stain grows wider at her shoulder. But her gait is steady and her eyes firm. When she reaches the top of the stairs she stares into my father's eyes. I am proud of her.*

"Sire, the road has been long, but I return your daughter to you at last." She kneels before him with sword extended and head bowed. With Margaret's help father walks over to her and puts his hand on her shoulder, staining his fingers with her blood.

"Arise, fine Abbess, for it's I who should kneel to ye. Ye have kept the spirit of Conall alive in me Deidre. Arise, Brigit, and embrace me."

The wounded pair are quite a sight, but their

warmth almost glows. The taste of victory is hardly sweet, but there is some solace in their dusty reunion.

Laegaire calls from below. The sweet spell of grace is broken.

"My king, come with me to the dungeon, quickly!"

A muddied and bloodied Colin climbs quickly to lend the king a hand down the scaffold to the courtyard. I twinge in empathy for their wounds as though the pain is mine.

I follow my father down the steps as Margaret stays with queen mum, who still is unsteady and lightheaded. Laegaire almost flies in front of us. His sword remains drawn and sparks sputter. Several guards quiver in the corners, hoping not to be seen. Morici brings up the rear. Culain stays to help Margaret with Macha for a minute and promises to follow soon.

As we approach the dark bowels of the dungeon, moans arise. The stench is foul, like cow dung covered with sweat. I cover my face. Morici draws me back, but I break free. I recognize the moans of the distorted man. It is Father Malachy. Or at least what is left of him. He has been stripped of all but a loincloth. The crusted blood from whippings covers his body. Leather straps stretch his arms and legs tautly. His eyes are pale and crusted. Only his whimpers and moans tell us he is alive. While others stand stunned, I rush to his side, sword drawn, and slash the leather thongs that bind him. A wail erupts from his throat. I dare not touch him for fear of giving him further pain.

"Father Malachy, it's me, Deidre. Shall we get you some balm?"

He waves me closer. His whisper is weak, but I strain to hear. His eyes are bloodied shut, but I see a weak smile on his face. Only I can hear him.

"Do you see him, Deidre?"

"Who, Father?" I whisper back and hold his hand.

"St. Michael, isn't he beautiful?" His smile broadens, but the pain makes him groan. "He says that he loves ye and that I will be within his arms soon." His smile broadens again. I yearn to see as he does, but I simply trust his vision.

As tears fill my eyes, I take his blue hand and implore, "Stay with us a while longer, Fr. Malachy, we need you."

He turns his head to me as though he could see. "You have Michael and Lugh." He coughs and frowns.

"Promise me one thing." His whispered breath is cold upon my ear.

"Anything, Father."

"Tell Culain to trust Lugh no matter what the King says." He coughs and grasps my hand with surprising firmness. His skin is thin and cold.

"I'll tell him, Father!" I know this means Fr. Malachy will not tell Culain himself. The words echo inside me like a banshee's wail.

"Good, my child, now I can join Michael." With that, he falls back and breathes his last. Pain no longer racks his limp body. I weep tears upon his wounds as I feel Laegaire drag me away. As I look up I see rage in Da's eyes.

"Brugh Donn will pay for his crimes. I'll have his head." Ice forms thickly on his face and chest. I know that I must share Malachy's words with Culain -- soon.

Anger and vengeance are quickly gathering their icy grip over my father's heart. My tears are as much for him as for Fr. Malachy. It saddens me that my love, as powerful as it is, cannot change the chaos around me.

I hear the King's raging screams bellow behind me. I cover my ears as he casts out threats and curses upon Brugh Donn and I feel his spittle spray on my arms.

As we return to the courtyard, Culain appears. I awkwardly hurry to him. He looks at me with bewilderment as I whisper to him: "Malachy's dead! He says to trust Lugh no matter what the King says." I know only Culain hears me, but I fear my own father, the High King of Eire. Confusion envelops me like a dark cloud. The chill of ice forms about my face. Culain puts his warm hands on my face and thaws the ice. His hands feel warm and soothing and I consider his eyes for guidance.

"Deidre, Lugh is always with us. Trust me." A few tears drip from the corners of my eyes as I hold his hand upon my face and I do trust him.

As we enter the courtyard, some guards already are taking down the scaffold. Fergus shouts orders. I know he has been captain of the Guard both for Brugh Donn and my father. Thick rope cinches Brugh Donn to a corner post. He is conscious, but dazed from his fall.

My father shouts hoarsely.

"Traitor of Eire! Coward! Murderer of priests! Ye're a disgrace to yer race."

He spits in Brugh Donn's face and is about to strike him when Brigit holds his hand like a vice.

"Remember, sire. You're a king. Act like one!" I share her sentiments.

He pulls his hand away and storms off. Brigit quickly walks to Laegaire.

"Guard the prisoner. The good king isn't himself."

A rising commotion swells. Father yells at Fergus.

"Who told ye to take down the gallows? Put them up again. Now! The sun will not set before Brugh Donn's execution."

"Yes, Sire." Fergus' face looks drawn as though his renewed allegiance to the king is no different than his allegiance to Brugh Donn. I am afraid he is right.

The King bellows again. I feel ashamed to be a Conall. The words are arrows to my heart.

"Fergus! We're too lenient with the prisoner. Put him on the rack!" Father's eyes glare with rage. Queen mum's face falls, or at least what is still visible. The ice looks as thick as ever. And father's face, when he turns around, is indistinguishable from when we first found him prisoner. My heart sinks and I feel coldness grip it. Suddenly I wish Martha and Caleb were here. I open my hands and feel the warmth of the quartz, feldspar, and granite. I put it over my heart and feel their presence.

"This can't be my father." I whisper out loud and Culain hears me.

He wraps his arm around me. "Trust in the Enchantment, Deidre." He shows me his stones and puts them to his heart. "Love transcends all."

Fergus unties Brugh Donn over the protest of Laegaire. Abbess Brigit comes to his side.

"Don't torture the prisoner, Fergus. Hasn't there been enough violence today?"

"Orders, ma'am. Orders of the High King himself!" Fergus keeps to his task.

Morgar strides over to the king, imploring clemency, but King Conchubar will not listen to him.

"Just be glad I'm not sending ye and that daughter of yers to the rack as well to pay for your crimes against Eire."

I had enough, Father or no Father, King or no King. I pull at his robe to get his attention.

"Morici and Morgar saved your life. How dare you threaten them so?"

The king raises his hand to strike me, but contains himself. I have no father.

"Deidre, these are the matters of men. Tend to the queen."

"I'll stay right here. You wouldn't be alive right now if it were not for each one of us. Laegaire, Brigit, Margaret, Colin, and yes, Morici and Morgar. I can't let you attack them."

"Cease your impudence, daughter. I'll hear no more of your prattle." He brushes me aside and tightens the leather thongs about Brugh Donn's wrists as Fergus wraps ropes about his arms. The darkness of the cloud cover is leaden. The same as my father's heart.

They lead Brugh Donn toward the dungeon.

Culain steps in front of them.

"You won't defile the kingship of Eire by harming this man!"

"Boy, he's a criminal. He deserves punishment." I see the King's anger rising. His patience is drawing thin.

"Culain, ye aren't yet man enough to understand."

"Conchubar, I understand that vengeance is your king right now. It isn't Tara or Eire or Danu that directs you."

The king raises his sword to the horror of all present. The gasps hold the king's arm.

"Indeed, ye are Sultain's son. A brave lad, Culain. But don't be a fool by challenging the High King."

"If I defeat Fergus, will you release Brugh Donn to me?"

Fergus and his guard laugh. Fergus soars nearly 7 feet tall. His biceps are as big as oaks. His barrel chest is strapped with armor and covered with heavy ice. Culain is not much taller than Fergus' belt buckle. They laugh and I shiver. What is my friend doing? What is my father doing? Have they gone mad?

Even the King joins the laugher.

"Fine joke, young Culain. Ye're no match for Fergus. Let us pass."

"Then I will take on all of you." The gasps rise again. My heart pounds with the speed of a hummingbird's wings.

"The boy needs a lesson, Fergus. Take care not to kill him." As the King turns his back upon Culain, my friend draws out his sword. It lights up the courtyard as though the sun sparks through it.

Fergus' laughter stops quickly and he draws his sword, twice the size and length of Culain's.

"Boy, this is no battle for the likes of ye! Let the criminal get his just rewards."

"Fergus, I tell you and the king, release the prisoner to me!"

Fergus laughs again.

I implore my friend, "He will have your head, Culain. Are you mad?" Sweat is swimming down my back and my throat is parched.

"It's time for the rage and vengeance to stop. It has no place in Ulster or Eire. I am here to engage all who proclaim hatred, even kings."

"Then you'll be another victim of vengeance, boy!"

Fergus' mighty swing would crush many a warrior, but it bounces off Culain's still sword as if it were made of rubber. Then Culain takes one quick swing with a flash of green streaking the air. Fergus's blade falls to the ground with a clang. Only the hilt remains. He steps back, surprised, and throws the handle down. He picks up a beam twice the size of Culain and swings it toward my friend's head. I clench my teeth and shut my eyes for a moment, fearing the worst.

"Can't you do better than that, Fergus?" I catch my breath as I see Culain's sword split the beam in two and it falls harmlessly to the ground, without even the slightest backward sway of Culain's body. He is like granite or quartz himself.

Another guard lunges at Culain to help his captain, but his sword suffers the same fate. The King picks up Margaret's sword that she had left on the ground.

"Fergus, take one of their enchanted swords. Be

done with him."

Being a sword of Lugh also, it cannot be cut by Culain. A sword fight ensues. Culain is too quick for Fergus to touch him and at each pass Culain strikes at a piece of armor. He is as lithe as a dancer and as quick as lightning. My friend indeed is earning my trust.

Finally, Culain cuts Fergus' central armor and it clatters off his chest. It exposes a hardened crust of ice. Culain slides to the side, cuts the ice without touching skin. No blood. No pain. But Fergus falls to his knees, feeling naked and subdued, no longer willing to fight. His guardsman helps him out of the way.

"Sire, it's time to turn the criminal over to me."

"I agreed to nothing, impish boy. I'll never release him to ye. Guards, seize him." As the King looks about him, every guard has a sword pointed to his neck by Laegaire, Brigit, Margaret (she has regained her sword), Colin, Morici, Morgar, and Ermanci. No one can move.

"Then I will do it myself!" The King lifts his sword and rushes Culain, but I rush in front of him, my sword sparkling aloft.

"Father, you'll have to come through me if you want Culain!"

I do not think. My sword shines even brighter than

Culain's. I have no fear.

My father raises his sword to strike, but an arm reaches out to grab it. Mum's arm. Her ice melts under the fire of her righteous anger.

"How dare ye lift a hand to yer daughter and the very people who saved us, Conchubar?" She rips the sword from his hand.

Macha glares at him as the last vestiges of ice melt from her face. "Release Brugh Donn to Culain. Now! There will be no more violence today!" Never have I been so proud of my mother. I hold my sword aloft and it glows in tribute to her.

The King stomps off to the castle womb. Macha turns to us.

"Deidre and Culain, as much as I yearn for reunion with ye, I bid ye take Brugh Donn away now, before Conchubar's rage destroys the very fabric of his kingdom. Go. Now!" Her words are wise but their truth weighs on my heart. To be separated again when we had only just saved them feels cruel. The pain is like needles to my heart.

Morici, Morgar, Brigit and Margaret join our side. Brigit holds the rope that binds Brugh Donn.

Laegaire shouts behind us.

"I'll stay here and plead your case to the King with Macha. Colin and Ermanci will stay with me and be my messengers to you. Remember, the power of the Enchantment runs strong in you. Seek Lugh. He'll guide your steps."

Our ragged band again separates from the Castle, the King and the Queen. Once again fear, hatred and vengeance separate me from my family. Again, I am an orphan, a lost child, but a child with the royal power of Lugh in my heart.

We need to flee to a place of safety. I look around at the dark leaden clouds. A change of power has not changed Doe castle. Only a change of heart can accomplish that feat. And the High King is not ready to change. I grab Culain's hands and stare into his eyes.

"You have a king's heart, Culain."

"And you a queen's, Deidre."

"What will we do?" I squeeze his hand as despair begins to frost my heart.

"Deidre, we'll return to the Forest and its Enchantment. There we'll truly be at home." Culain puts his arm on my shoulder as we trudge across the drawbridge and into the green of the forest.

"When will we bring the Enchantment to the rest

of Eire, Culain?"

"We must find Lugh and ask him."

I look back with tired eyes and an aching heart. I feel the stones in my palm.

"Can we stop at St. Michael's, Culain?"

"Yes, Deidre, the parents we abandoned are there."

A large bird rises over the forest. Its wingspan is too great to be a hawk. It is a grand bald eagle. Its wings spread as wide as Maeve's. It soars with grace and beauty ever higher. The sun's rays break through behind it and I hear the music, Lugh's tune. I wipe the tear from my eye and point to the eagle. Culain smiles.

"Our quest isn't over, Deidre. The light of Lugh will shine again at Doe Castle."

As heavy as my heart feels, the eagle lifts it a little

higher.

Gabrielle whispers in my ear. "Trust your love."

I feel it.

Do you?

The End

Acknowledgements

In Book 1, **Deidre's Dawn,** I acknowledged the gift my young children gave by asking me to share my imagination in bedtime stories. My wife Barbara encouraged the practice (shared parenting) and kept my storytelling spark alive! These days it is my grandchildren Owen and Olivia, avid readers both, that are excited about my writing and keep me motivated.

I credit The Institute of Children's Literature in Connecticut for giving me my first opportunity in the 1990s to test my creative writing skills with published authors/teachers in correspondence courses for short story and novel writing. I thank Teri Martini and Kevin McColley for their editing guidance in writing **Deidre's Dawn** and **Rising Darkness**.

I am grateful to my massage school classmate of the late '90s, Eldonna Edwards, who was an early fellow aspiring writer who supported my desire to become an author. After moving to California, she shared writing prompts with me from her Central Coast writers group (which led me to start my local group at Barnes and Noble). My good friend "Ellie" published her true-life story *Lost in Transplantation, Memoir of an Unconventional Organ Donor* in 2014. Her debut novel, *This I Know* releases in 2018.

I again must acknowledge my fellow writers in my monthly "Writer's Exchange" group at Muskegon's Barnes and Noble, especially the "regulars" Samm Bogner, John Cox, Anita Harms, Michele May, and Ron Robothom. I am resident "Prompter" for our lively adventures into spontaneous, creative writing sessions which dates back to May of 1999. We all support each other in our forays into writing and publishing.

I also tip my hat to the members of my men's group for their patience and acceptance of my exuberance in reading draft chapters of my book aloud at some of our meetings. Thanks for your tolerance and encouragement, David Bernstein, Charlie Donaldson, Girbe Eefsting, Bruce Klein, and Jim Persoon.

More recently, my fellow authors at Argon Press took me under their wing, encouraged me to get serious about publishing and provided excellent guidance. So, I thank Steve LeBel, Deanna J. Compton, Ingar Rudholm, J. Scott Payne, C.J. Coombes and H. William Ruback for their steady support. You may see some of us together at book signings in West Michigan!

Thanks to Deanna J. Compton for her assistance with the cover design with some help from H. Wiliam Ruback. Thanks to all the artists who provided the chapter illustration images via shutterstock.com.

Once again, thanks to British Symbolist artist Edward Robert Hughes, whose pre-Raphaelite water-color painting "Twilight Fantasy" (1911) graces the cover of this book. His magical art inspired *The Enchantment* series.

Five-star praise for **Book 1 of The Enchantment Series**

"**Deidre's Dawn** takes the reader on a delightful adventure. Deidre is filled with life-force energy… alive and strong despite her oppressive environment. This story is for people of all ages, especially those who appreciate the mythical and magical realm of life…something we all need right now in our high-tech, fast-paced society." *-- Laura Grace, Ph.D., Lecturer, Author and Founder of the Circle of Grace in Central Coast California*

"**Deidre's Dawn** is a delightful story of a young girl in ancient Ireland. Deidre and her friend Culain find themselves drawn into a land of enchantment and mystery as they seek to avoid abusive homes and discover the truth about their past. The story is fun for children, but adults will enjoy it, too. The story is told by Deidre in a wonderful style that offers rich and compelling descriptions especially as their journey leads them into the Enchanted Forest. I especially liked Gabrielle and Nacham; they were brilliant and unique and worth the entire story by itself." *-- Steve LeBel, Author of* **The Universe Builders** *Series*

How about _you_? *Share your impression of* **Rising Darkness!**
Leave a review *on Amazon.com so others may enjoy the adventures of Deidre and Culain in The Enchantment.*
Go to www.amazon.com, select Books and enter the title,
Rising Darkness: Book 2 of The Enchantment
Scroll down, click "Write a customer review"

Author J. Michael McFadden lives by the Lake Michigan beach in Muskegon, MI with his wife Barbara, where brilliant sunsets and frothing waves inspire his writing imagination. **Deidre's Dawn,** his debut novel, takes place in ancient Ireland, home of the legends and lore of his ancestors. **Rising Darkness** reveals more of the saga of Deidre and Culain in **Book 2** of **The Enchantment** trilogy. **Book 3** chapters dance like fairies in his mind as **Star Lights** evolves as the compelling conclusion of **The Enchantment** Series.

Made in the USA
Middletown, DE
27 November 2018